THE LOVE IN EURO

Book 2

PARIS

Sofia di Siena

Published by Sofia di Siena

© 2020 Paris

All rights reserved. No part of this book may be reproduced or modified in any form, including photocopying, recording, or by any information storage and retrieval system, without permission in writing from the publisher.

The scanning, uploading and distribution of this book without permission is a theft of the author's intellectual property. If you would like permission to use material from the book please contact : sofiadisiena777@gmail.com

Disclaimer:
This is a work of fiction. Many of the names, places, characters and incidents are either the product of the author's imagination or are used fictitiously. Any resemblance to actual organizations, events, locales or persons — living or dead — is entirely coincidental.
© 2020.

For C

▲

PARIS

CONTENTS

Chapter 1 ▲ THE CITY OF LIGHT

Chapter 2 ▲ LE JARDIN DES TUILERIES

Chapter 3 ▲ THE EIFFEL TOWER

Chapter 4 ▲ SAINT VALENTINE'S DAY

Chapter 5 ▲ PARISIAN NIGHT

Chapter 6 ▲ THE BOIS DE BOULOGNE

Chapter 7 ▲ THE SECRET

Chapter 8 ▲ AU REVOIR

Chapter 9 ▲ LYON

Chapter 10 ▲ MONACO

Chapter 11 ▲ ZEUS ARRIVES HOME

Chapter 12 ▲ THE VILLA

Chapter 13 ▲ A NIGHT IN TUSCANY

Chapter 14 ▲ ARRIVEDERCI … THE SECOND GOODBYE

CHAPTER ONE

▲

THE CITY OF LIGHT

'Paris is always a good idea' ... Audrey Hepburn

February 12

Maria got into the private chauffeured car that she had arranged to meet her at Paris Charles de Gaulle airport. She had booked the car and driver for the whole week. It was February, late afternoon and it was raining in Paris, but even this grey rainy day could not dim the beauty of the ancient city. As they drove in from CDG through the more industrial outskirts, with its high-rise apartment buildings, towards the centre of the beautiful old city Maria just stared at the architecture, each boulevard prettier than the next. After delays leaving JFK she could not wait to just flop onto her king size bed in her suite at her five star hotel just off the Champs-Elysées, before exploring all the places she had been researching for weeks. She was so excited.

After two years of separation her lengthy divorce had been finalised two months earlier. She had promised herself this trip to Paris, alone, to give herself some 'me time' before returning to New York to decide what she was going to do in the next stage of her life. She didn't need to work, her divorce from James had treated her generously, but there was no way she was going to be a lady who lunched, as the English put it, she was going to start her own business. She just didn't know what yet. She had a desire to help other women, but *how* exactly she was yet to find out. She didn't know whether to try and start a business directly helping empower other women, or to create a successful business that allowed her to donate to women's start-ups and charities. Whatever she did, she believed if you had the good fortune to be well off in this world, you had a duty to give something back.

They drove into the centre of Paris, up Boulevard Haussmann and Maria saw the Arc de Triomphe approaching. The driver, Charles, who had taken to this American lady who spoke some French, was taking her the scenic route and circled it twice so she could get a good look at the monument that guarded the tomb of the unknown soldier from WW1. To the north west, looking down Avenue de la Grande Armée, Maria could see the business district of La Défense. They turned down the Champs-Elysées and Maria felt such a feeling of happiness that she had finally come back to Paris after so many years. The Louvre museum she knew was at the other end of the long tree-lined avenue. The traffic was busy, with bikes and cars regularly blowing their horns at tourists dodging the traffic lights and standing in the middle of the avenue to get a perfect straight shot of the Arc de Triomphe from a distance.

They turned down rue George V, passing the flagship Louis Vuitton store on the corner and the car stopped outside the beautiful hotel. Charles opened the door "Madame" and smiled admiringly at her. Maria was used to men smiling at her, and receiving admiring looks. She had long dark hair, blue eyes, perfect make up and, although recently it had been lacking, a beautiful smile. She was tall and athletic looking, the sort of woman any ballgown looked good on. She was approaching 50 but nobody ever guessed her true age. She passed for around 40 according to most guesses, and recently 37 (although that particular admirer had been in his 20's she remembered with a naughty smile!). She took pride in taking care of herself, went to the gym regularly, and was a beauty treatment and cosmetics addict. Her daughters, Luisa and Carla, were constantly borrowing her latest Guerlain nail polish, Dior lipstick or Chanel eyeshadow palette! As if they didn't have enough make-up of their own! The years of sport, regular facials and expensive beauty products had proved their worth though, Maria was stunningly beautiful, naturally, with no surgery or treatments, although people often asked if she had had work done.

There was a black Italian-plated 4X4 Maserati parked outside the hotel, and Maria had the peculiar sensation it seemed to be moving or rocking on its own. As she entered the lobby of the hotel, she could hear a heated conversation going on at reception. A tall dark-haired man with his back to her was explaining to a reluctant receptionist in broken French then accented English that yes, he had checked prior to arriving that his dog was welcome. The fact that the hotel had not specified they meant "handbag" dogs was not his fault, and in any case, he did not believe that was correct. The man demanded to speak to the manager. Although his English was good, from his accent the man was clearly Italian, and even if he had not said a word, Maria would have guessed he was Italian by his perfectly cut Armani (she was sure it was) suit.

Maria was greeted by another receptionist and asked about room service breakfast timings while checking in. She intended to go for an early morning run before breakfast - start her new life as she meant to go on, wasting no time and taking care of SELF! This vacation she had banned herself from thinking about guys. This was a self-rediscovery trip.

Charles had brought her luggage in from the car and Maria confirmed with him when he would pick her up tomorrow before he left. The large bag was half empty as she intended to buy some things while she was here.

She was so excited to have a guided driving tour around Paris before lunch tomorrow. She liked to walk around cities, but while recovering from the long journey, tomorrow a drive seemed a much better idea. Charles had also recommended that he should take her to the stunning Place Vendôme, where he would wait with all the other drivers of luxury cars, while their occupants shopped exclusively at Piaget, Van Cleef & Arpels, Chanel, Dior, Buccellati, the list went on. Of course, Maria had heard of all the places he was going to take her to, the Sacré-Coeur, Notre-Dame cathedral, the Louvre and of course the Eiffel Tower, etc, but this was her first trip to Paris in decades. James had always been so busy with work; their vacations had been mainly spent in the Caribbean or Hawaii. He had not been particularly interested in travelling to Europe. Maria had spent six months working as an au pair south of Paris when she was 20 and she still spoke a bit of French. She had missed Europe all these years. It was hard to believe she had spent nearly twenty years with James before his affair with his lawyer colleague pushed Maria to file for divorce. He had had an affair with Emily, a colleague who was British, from London. James was actually American/Dutch nationality, more for ease of travel for work than visiting, as his immediate family all now lived in the States. Their daughters had Dutch and American passports.

Maria jumped as there was a very loud, very low, bark behind her! She turned around to see what could only be described as an over excited horse wagging its tail and wiggling (if such a large creature could wiggle) being brought in, greeting the Italian guest as if it had not seen him for days.

"D'accordo d'accordo Zeus, OK Zeus" the man said, as the dog, an enormous grey Great Dane with pale green eyes whacked its tail energetically against Maria's leg. "I am so sorrrrry" the man apologised. Maria laughed and the man looked relieved, she sensed he was more used to people being frightened of his pet.

"No problem" she said, "I have one just the same at home, except she is a girl!". Bella was at home with her daughters while Maria was away.

As she explained this to the man, she noticed for the first time how incredibly good looking he was. She was certain she had guessed about the Armani suit correctly and the rest of him was straight off a catwalk. He was very tall, had quite long wild-looking dark hair, was slightly unshaven and had very intense dark brown eyes. His features were angular with an aquiline nose and pronounced chin, but in a male model-look kind of way. She guessed he was early to mid-forties.

"My name is Alexander Sabatini" he said and reached out his hand, which Maria shook.

"Sono Maria Rossi" she said, which seemed to unnerve him, realising this American woman might speak his language!

"You have an Italian name, but you are American?" he could not help but ask.

"My father was from Argentina, with Italian ancestry, it's a bit complicated" Maria said with a smile but didn't tell him that until two months ago she had been Maria Rossi Smythe-Janssen and was celebrating her divorce from one of New York's top lawyers.

He had very large hands and a nice firm handshake, and she felt a frisson of attraction as he held on to her hand for slightly longer than was necessary and looked at her with his intense eyes.

Maria had decided she was absolutely staying away from men, certainly for this trip and preferably for at least the next few months. Although she had dated on and off in the last couple of years, she wanted time to sort out her new life with no distractions. In any case James had put her off anything too serious with the male race. She had to admit though, this Italian was stunningly handsome.

"Alexander is not an Italian name" Maria pointed out.

"Yeees my mother wanted a strong name and she didn't like 'Alessandro' the Italian version, so she got her way!" he laughed.

"But people normally call me Xander" he explained in his gorgeous Italian accent, looking at her intensely.

The manager of the hotel arrived just at that moment apologising profusely and Alexander's attention was taken away "mi scusi" he said smiling at Maria. As the largest dog bed she had ever seen (bigger even than her own dear Bella's) was brought in, Maria made her way past them to the elevator; she felt the Italian stranger's eyes on her and when she looked round he was staring at her. How gorgeous he was and how funny he had the same race of dog that she had! For some reason Perdy and Perdita, the dalmations from 101 Dalmations popped into her mind, their owners had met because of the dogs. She immediately banished such stupid thoughts from her mind and made her way into the ornate elevator. You are OFF men Maria, she said to herself sternly. Maria loved dogs and horses, but her one dream, which did not fit at all with living in an apartment in Manhattan, was to have a macaw. She had always adored birds, especially the blue macaws, and one day *"when she lived in a house in the country"* she always told herself with a laugh, she would get one or two. She had always had a dog though, and Bella was such a funny character, Danes were humanlike. She stepped out of the elevator and made her way down the corridor.

The suite was absolutely stunning as she had expected, with the highest quality bed linens and furnishings. The balcony had a view over the rooftops towards the Eiffel Tower. She went into the bathroom and immediately could not wait to shower after the long journey. The entirely marble tiled multi-shower was chilling heaven.

Once she had unpacked her clothes and put them away in the ample sized wardrobe, she turned on the shower and waited a moment for it to heat. Then she took off all her clothes she had travelled in and stepped in. She soaped herself sensually all over then used a fine body scrub on her arms, legs and butt. Long distance travel always makes you feel so grubby, she thought. The pressure of the water on her skin felt sensual and relaxing at the same time. Maria liked to feel smooth all over, even if there was nobody to appreciate the exquisite shape or feel of her body right now. She felt confident knowing her body was pampered, like an Egyptian queen. She caressed her breasts and flat stomach as her hands moved down slowly with the water between her legs. As she soaped herself sensually Maria's mind wandered to the man she had seen in the lobby, it had been a while since she had been with a man and he was the most attractive she had seen for a long time. She washed her hair and just stood under the water for a long time, letting the pressure ease the tension from her shoulders.

It was already getting dark, so she put on a white towelling robe and ordered a glass of champagne with a delicious sounding club sandwich from room service. She lay on the bed and checked her cell phone while she waited.

When the spectacular club sandwich arrived, she sipped her glass of champagne and silently congratulated herself on following her dream and actually making it here. She stared out of the window at the Parisian rooftops, with the top of the Eiffel Tower and the dark tower of Montparnasse visible in the distance. The balcony at this time of year was just a little bit too cold, otherwise she would have sat outside for a while.

One day she would come back in the summertime she promised herself. She could already feel the vibe of the city. She adored NYC and would probably always live there, but she had always been so drawn to Paris, Madrid, Rome, Venice and all the other beautiful European cities. One day she would visit them too. Right now she was escaping in Paris.

▲▲▲

CHAPTER TWO

▲

LE JARDIN DES TUILERIES

February 13

Maria got up at 6am, ignored the jet lag, she didn't have time for that, and put on her running gear before she could talk herself out of going outside in the drizzle. Even for someone who loved running and sport, it sometimes took a lot of effort to actually start. She normally used the stern talking-to voice in her head to tell herself that if she wanted a body of a 35 year old, with a pert booty and no cellulite then you have to MOVE THAT BOOTY. She only had a week here and her plan with the early start was to kick the jetlag immediately so as not to waste any of the mornings here. She promised herself she would book an all over body massage in the hotel spa later as a reward for her planned 10K this morning. She had already seen the tempting list of treatments with the gorgeous and extremely expensive beauty products. As a special prize because it was raining and for being dedicated to fitness, she also decided she would treat herself to some new running gear. She reminded herself that every small achievement should be celebrated, which meant a good excuse for shopping. She was determined to get herself into her new "Queen" mentality, take care of herself after her divorce and basically take no shit from anyone.

She strapped her music to her arm, tied her hair back, put on her visor and made her way down to the lobby. The reception staff greeted her, and she smiled at them and said "bonjour", before going out onto the avenue George V. She decided to turn right out of the hotel and make her way down to the Seine, then run along the bank for 5km before turning back. As she ran past the beautiful bridges and buildings, she started to feel really excited about this new stage in her life, where SHE had total control and was not answerable to any man! She was not alone at 6am, a large number of Parisians ran along the Seine in the early morning, before the pollution started to rise with the heavy traffic later in the day.

Just under an hour later she got back, hot and happily sweaty. She noticed the Maserati outside the hotel again with its back door open and fleetingly thought it was a shame if the handsome Italian had only been there for one night.

She decided to take the stairs to avoid being trapped in the elevator with anyone – although she looked sexy in her tight running outfit, a potentially hot sweaty smell is not attractive. She was heading towards the stairs when she heard the elevator open just behind her and the woman who had been waiting for it give a loud squeak of alarm. Amused, Maria watched as Zeus the Great Dane, followed by his owner came out of the elevator. The woman looked absolutely terrified and quickly stepped inside before the dog got close to her. Zeus was clearly being taken for his morning walk and was boisterous. That explained why the car was there she thought. He barked at Maria, and Alexander looked round to see what was attracting his dog. He looked very pleased to see her, smiled and said "buongiorno", not very subtly looking her up and down with his lovely dark brown eyes. Maria smiled back, returned the greeting and continued up the stairs to her much-deserved shower.

She got into her room, stretched for twenty minutes, then undressed and put the shower on. The overhead drop shower had great pressure and she used the side jets to massage her legs and butt. The touch of the water felt sexy to her and she suddenly wondered what the Italian would look like, wet and naked in his shower, his muscular arms reaching up to run his hands over his face and through his wet black hair, like a men's perfume advert. *NO Maria,* she caught herself, stop behaving like a 17 year old and concentrate. She soaped herself, then shaved her legs and pussy. She was bikini ready every day of the year, her fingernails and toenails were a semi-permanent red, especially for this trip. Maria believed you should always look your best; just because you take care of your appearance does not mean you are an airhead, it is possible to be a make-up addict, look your best AND be an intelligent person.

After a huge breakfast in her suite, of fruit followed by a full English breakfast as she was absolutely famished, Maria got dressed in jeans, black hoody and a New York Knicks black cap. She was looking forward to relaxing in the car and taking in the beautiful Parisian architecture. She called down to the spa and booked her massage for later that day, then sent a message to Luisa and Carla, who were no doubt still sleeping in their Manhattan apartment near Central Park. It would still be night in NYC at the moment. She hoped everything was fine at home, the girls had admitted planning a "small" party.

Maria went downstairs, reprimanding herself silently for being disappointed the Italian was not in the lobby this time, met Charles and went out to the car.

They drove away from the hotel towards the iconic Champs-Elysées and Maria remembered a history book she had read recently, which had showed black and white photos of lines and lines of German soldiers marching down the Champs-Elysées during the Second World War. Then she recalled watching the end of the Tour de France cycle race which always ended in Paris with the riders circling the Champs-Elysées before the exciting sprint finish in front of packed spectators lining the avenue. Charles was a great tour guide, he gave Maria information about the different areas of central Paris they drove through, in French simple enough for her to understand.

They headed for the Cathédrale du Sacré-Coeur and Montmartre first. Maria walked slowly around Montmartre and ended up in Place du Tertre with its hundreds of talented artists, all painting portraits of visitors or working on their current canvas, to sell to tourists. She stopped and had a coffee while watching the painters at work. After a while she made her way through a couple of narrow streets and arrived from the rear of the Sacré-Coeur (or cathedral of the Sacred Heart). After admiring it from the front, as it seemed to glow pure white despite the cloudy weather, she went into the enormous cathedral. The quiet serenity inside was such a contrast to the bustling streets she had just been through. The marble sculptures, paintings and stained-glass windows were truly breathtaking. She sat down in a pew at the back for ten minutes and just sat there, being in the present moment, allowing the stillness to calm her mind.

Charles had told Maria he would wait in a back street at the bottom of the hill below the Sacré-Coeur, so after admiring the incredible view over Paris to the south from in front of the cathedral she made her way down the hundreds of steps. On the way down there were the usual street sellers of sparkly Eiffel towers, keyrings, "designer" handbags of questionable origin and numerous nick-nacks to tempt the tourists. She headed down through the narrow streets, full of gift shops selling t-shirts adorned with Parisian landmarks, Notre-Dame fridge magnets and a million other things to tempt you, and eventually found Charles waiting in the car.

They drove for what seemed like miles as the traffic made it seem longer, each street and avenue held photo opportunities at every corner, they were so classically beautiful. Every street had cafés full of chic looking people, having coffee and watching the world go by.

They drove through the 10th and then the 3rd arrondissements (or neighborhoods) and back to the River Seine where Maria could see renovations ongoing at the Cathédrale Notre-Dame de Paris. They stopped briefly and Maria walked into the courtyard and admired the front of the cathedral with its beautiful circular stained-glass window. From there they circled back through the Latin Quarter and crossed back over the Seine over the Pont Alexandre III with its ornate gold design details and art nouveau lamps. They drove along the banks of the Seine and then turned back towards the Champs-Elysées down the rue de Rivoli, in the 1st arrondissement, passing the Louvre museum on their left. It is the largest museum in the world and Maria planned to spend half a day there later in the week.

As they continued on down past Le Jardin des Tuileries (or Tuileries Garden) that links the Louvre with Place de la Concorde, Maria couldn't believe her eyes. Amongst the many people out enjoying the gardens, many with chihuahuas or similar sized dogs, she saw the unmistakeable Zeus, accompanied by his equally impressive master. Maria made a quick decision, surreptitiously checked her makeup and asked Charles to pull into a side street and wait for her. He turned up rue de Castiglione and Maria got out, crossed back over rue de Rivoli and entered the gardens.

She suddenly thought to herself *OMG what am I going to say to him? Shall I make him think I was just walking in the gardens by chance? If I say I saw him and then stopped, he'll think I am a stalker or at the very least a bit forward.* She couldn't decide, so she just started walking towards the circular fountain at the end of the gardens and hoped he might spot her. She started taking pictures of the view beyond the Place de la Concorde, up the Champs-Elysées to the Arc de Triomphe in the distance.

"Mariiia?" she heard a familiar accented voice ask and her heart leapt.

She turned and Alexander was approaching, with Zeus walking to heel, less boisterous than the last time she saw him. Xander was trying to contain his pleasure at seeing Maria again, he had been hoping that they would meet again, and he wanted to ask her to have a drink with him. He was on a strictly business visit to Paris but was recently single having broken up with yet another girlfriend, after being divorced a couple of years previously. It had not ended well, and he had not intended to get involved or indeed pursue any woman for at least a couple of months, but against his better judgement Maria had got his attention in a big way...

"Hi again Alexander, how are you?"

"How nice to see you again" he said, staring at her "do you want to walk up to the Louvre with me? And please call me Xander".

They chatted about the weather, the architecture, the fact that Maria had a Great Dane as well, all the while glancing at each other and holding eye contact for just that little bit longer than normal. As they approached the Louvre and crossed over into the Cour de

Napoléon they admired the stunning Palais de Louvre museum, originally a palace where various kings of France had lived when they spent time in Paris. The entrance, the famous glass pyramid which had caused so much uproar in 1989 when it first opened, had now become a famous landmark in itself. It had caused huge controversy not just because of its modern design but also because the architect had been Chinese-American and not French.

"So, tell me Maria, what are you doing in Paris?"

"Well, actually, I am treating myself, I just got divorced and I have escaped for a week!" she half smiled and rolled her eyes slightly, as if to convey the stress of the last couple of years in a few seconds.

"Oh oh I understand, I am divorced also" Xander said, understanding immediately.

When Maria said she was divorced Xander surprised himself at the strength of his pleasure that this stunning woman was actually free. He had assumed she must be married. He explained to Maria that he was here meeting a client to finalise the architects' plans for an office block outside Firenze as the French company were expanding into Italy.

Maria was trying to behave normally and with poise, but just walking next to him she was acutely aware of him. She could smell his perfume, Dior Sauvage. She couldn't remember the last time a man had had this strong an effect on her, so quickly.

As they admired the beautiful museum, they were both entranced by the sense of history. The building was originally started in the 12th century as Louvre Castle and remains of the mediaeval foundations are preserved under the Sully wing. Maria loved history and found this fascinating. Xander totally shared her love of history and historical sites and they smiled at each other, both intuitively feeling that it seemed as though they had known each other for a long time, and had not only met just yesterday.

"Would you like to have a drink in the hotel bar tonight?" Xander suddenly asked Maria "I have a client dinner later tonight, but we could meet at 19.00, if you are free of course?" he said giving her a wide smile.

Maria stared at him, he was gorgeous, with his Italian dark good looks, sensual mouth and perfect teeth. She had had many a discussion with her girlfriends about how you should never trust a man who doesn't have good teeth. They always joked about it when considering possible boyfriends for the single ones amongst the group of close-knit friends, which at the moment were herself, Lisette and Luke. She smiled to herself as she agreed to meet later.

"That would be really nice" Maria smiled.

They walked all the way back down through the Tuileries Garden, past the fountain and on to Place de la Concorde. They joked about getting one of the "rickshaw" style bicycle taxis that will pedal you dangerously around the huge, cobbled roundabout with its fountains and obelisk and up the Champs-Elysées.

"I don't think he would like Zeus on the seat!" Xander laughed.

They both laughed and Maria asked Xander to take a picture of her with the Luxor obelisk and the Champs-Elysées behind her. Then she took one of him and promised to send it to him later. For a second it seemed totally normal to be taking snaps of each other in front of famous places in Paris. They talked again about the history in Paris. Place de la Concorde is the biggest square in Paris measuring an enormous 19 hectares. Originally, in 1755, it had been named Place Louis XV, honouring the King at the time, and there used to be an equestrian statue of him in pride of place. During the French revolution in 1789, the statue was ripped down and demolished by the people, and the square was re-named Place de la Révolution. The brand new government formed by the revolutionists placed a guillotine in the middle of the square and, among many other aristocrats, they beheaded Louis XVI there in 1793. Maria wondered what life would have been like back then, with the impoverished people of France in the middle of overthrowing their royal family who had ruled for centuries.

They talked about the central monument, the Luxor Obelisk, which has been in the centre of the square since 1836. It was one of two obelisks adorned with hieroglyphics that had sat at the entrance to the Luxor Temple in Egypt, and both were gifted to France by Egypt. It is over 3000 years old, weighs over 250 tonnes and is the only one of the twin obelisks which was actually transported to France. The second obelisk stayed in Egypt and was eventually, in the 1990s, gifted back to the Egyptians by President François Mitterand.

It was not busy, being February, so Maria and Xander went across the cobbled road to the centre of the square to have a closer look; the obelisk sits on a huge base with plaques that describe how the enormous object was brought to France, back in the 1830s.

Xander asked if she had seen the Les Misérables stage show which was set during the French revolution.

"Oh yes of course" Maria exclaimed, remembering the show most people called "Les Miz" for short, that she had seen on Broadway. Now she was actually standing on the very earth on which all the bloodshed had happened, in Paris, so long ago.

"I dreamed a dream of times gone by …." Xander started singing one of the famous songs from the show.

Maria laughed then very quickly realised Xander had an incredible singing voice! As he continued, seemingly not really caring about the few other tourists who could hear him, Maria just stared at him.

" ... I had a dream my life would be, so different from this hell I'm li-iii-ving" he stopped eventually and looked at her, smiling.

"Oh sorrrry I hope I did not embarrass you, I am Italian, we love singing" he grinned as two of the nearby tourists attempted unsuccessfully to hide the fact they had been videoing him on their phones. He was probably already hashtagged #crazyitaliansinger!

Maria laughed again and was impressed at how brave he was singing in public. She would never have the courage to do that. They both looked at each other and laughed out loud.

"You are so beautiful when you smile Maria" he gazed at her.

"I am definitely going to see the show again as soon as I can" Maria replied and they exchanged a long look, both of them thinking the same thing.

Xander could picture himself as if it were happening now, sat in a theatre with this beautiful woman next to him, in the darkened audience, watching Les Misérables tell the story of that tumultuous time in Paris as the common people of France finally got sick of their ruling class living in luxury, while they died of starvation.

Maria was imagining the same scenario, although she could not think where or when this could possibly happen, and she once again told herself to stop acting like such a silly teenager.

They waited for a gap in the traffic then they started to cross back over the road. As they did so, Xander reached for her hand and held it firmly. Maria found this so protective and felt her heart beat faster at his touch; his hand was strong with nice smooth skin. It brought back memories of when she had always grasped her daughters' hands to cross the road, many years ago.

"Remember crossing the road with kids" she reminisced "thankfully they are all grown up now and self-sufficient. I did love it when my girls were small but it's nice to be so free now".

A shadow suddenly crossed Xander's face, and his eyes became guarded, just for a second, before returning to normal.

"Oh yes of course I do" he said quickly.

"But having young kids was a VERY long time ago now!" she said.

Xander looked away very quickly, which Maria noticed but could not pinpoint why she sensed he was uneasy, and they stopped a little further on.

He kissed her on the cheek when they said goodbye. The same frisson of anticipation ran through Maria as he touched her cheek lightly and she caught the scent of his Dior Sauvage perfume again. Xander tried to control his excitement at seeing her later, but inside he was feeling like he was an 18 year old going on a hot date with the most popular girl in class.

Maria watched Xander walk off, with passersby commenting on Zeus "il est magnifique" "quel beau chien", what a gorgeous dog, she had exactly the same reactions in NYC with Bella. She walked back around to rue de Rivoli, found Charles and asked him to take her to Place Vendôme, she was in the mood to buy something and one of her dream home accessories shops was located there.

Place Vendôme is a beautiful classic 'square' (actually octagonal) with ancient buildings. King Louis XIV commissioned the square and had a statue in his honour in the centre, but in 1810 Napoleon replaced it with the current, and very photogenic now it has turned a pretty turquoise colour, bronze central column which is formed from 1,200 enemy cannons!

They stopped outside Chanel, behind a large number of Bentley and Mercedes private cars and their waiting drivers. Maria got out and went into the boutique. There was a dazzling array of choice, and the intricate workmanship of all their pieces was a pleasure in itself, just to look at.

Maria admired their tanzanite collection, drawn to the intense blue-purple colour of the gems. She chose a tanzanite pendant and a pearl necklace with a lion detail in white gold set with diamonds. She liked the idea of the lion, she had felt for several years that she had had to be a lioness to save her own sanity and create a new life, all the while raising two teenage girls. Now she had finally done it and she was taking the first tentative steps in her new future. Leaving Chanel, she walked across to Buccellati and after gazing at all their beautiful creations, bought a set of three solid silver, intricately detailed photo frames.

Once she got back to the hotel, Maria immediately went to the wardrobe and tried to decide what to wear when she met Xander in the bar later. She decided on a simple but well-fitting Roberto Cavalli dress that showed off her figure while still being very classy, with leather knee-high heeled boots. She then changed into her sports clothes as she had her appointment at the spa in the hotel for a full body massage.

The spa was sheer bliss, luxury wherever you looked. Maria just lay on the massage table in the dim light and let the masseuse take care of all the tightness in her muscles. The products smelt absolutely gorgeous, so calming and sensual. She lay listening to the sounds of a rainforest; a stream gurgling slowly, rain dripping through the leaves and exotic birds calling ... macaws she thought ... she switched off, she felt so relaxed the hour and a half massage seemed to be over very quickly.

▲▲▲

CHAPTER THREE

▲

THE EIFFEL TOWER

February 13 ... later that evening

Maria left her room and went down in the elevator. She felt confident in her dress and her body felt so good and tension free thanks to the massage earlier.

She walked in and glanced around the bar, attracting admiring glances from several men who were sat at tables, with their wives or not, they still stared. Her eyes found Alexander sat at the bar waiting for her. Her heart gave a jolt and she told herself inwardly to calm down right now. He was wearing a suit as he had a business dinner later, but he had taken off the jacket. His dark skin and hair were set off to perfection by the expensive white shirt he was wearing. Once again, he smelled luscious, his perfume mixed with the unmistakeable just-showered male smell. She tried not to make it too obvious she had checked out his muscular shoulders and impressive chest, his shirt slightly open at the neck. He looked her up and down not hiding his appreciation of her choice of dress.

"Maria, do you realise how many men stare at you, wherever you go?" he asked, touching her arm as he kissed her on the cheek "you look very beautiful tonight" he said, and then "is that a Roberto Cavalli dress?"

"Oh, no not really" she said "and yes it is" she smiled, this guy knew his Italian designers and although she had not noticed who was looking at her, she was quietly pleased he seemed to be making sure they knew she was with him.

"What would you like to drink?" he asked her.

Xander was drinking Perrier as he had his meeting later and he never drank before business, not even during a business dinner, but Maria suddenly fancied a cocktail.

"You know Xander I really fancy a pina colada, even though they are a beach holiday type drink!" she laughed.

He ordered one for her and they chatted briefly. Xander's cell phone rang suddenly, and he excused himself and left the bar. Maria watched him walk out, he had such athletic grace. She took a sip of her cocktail and it was exquisite, she realised with a start that she felt really happy and relaxed for the first time in a VERY long time. Stress and worry had become her normal for the last couple of years and this new feeling was very noticeable and very pleasant, although at the same time she was shocked she could not remember when she last felt this relaxed. When you are coping with a bad situation, she thought, it goes on for so long you become accustomed to feeling anxious most of the time. She took another sip of her cocktail and savoured the feeling.

Alexander walked elegantly back into the bar five minutes later with a contemplative look on his face.

"So that was my client, they have pushed the dinner tonight to tomorrow lunchtime" he said looking carefully at her, "I have an idea".

Maria looked at him and that same feeling deep within her returned as they looked into each other's eyes.

"So, what is your idea?" she asked.

"How about thiiiiis" he said in his adorable accent "we go to the Eiffel Tower from here and watch the lights at 20.00, then, would you like to have dinner with me?" Xander asked.

The Eiffel Tower, after dark, lights up with a sparkling light show for five minutes, on the hour every hour.

Suddenly the idea of going to the Eiffel Tower in Paris, at night, standing close to this unbelievably handsome Italian man to watch the lights, was the best idea she had heard for a long time.

"That sounds like a great idea, let's do that" she smiled at him.

"OK great, so we can finish our drinks then go across to the Trocadero and watch from there" he said, pronouncing it Trocadeerrrro.

"I will call Charles, it will be easier to let him drop us off and then wait somewhere before taking us to a restaurant for dinner, what do you think? Is that OK with you?" Maria asked.

"Of course, we could take my Maserati but yes your car would be better" Xander agreed.

They finished their drinks while chatting about a hundred and one things. Alexander's English really was excellent, and they found they had many things in common; they both loved sport and keeping fit; they were both interested in personal growth and spirituality; they both loved the outdoors. Xander even liked horseback riding which Maria had planned to restart this year as part of her new life. As he was telling her about riding horses back in Tuscany in Italy when he was younger, she had a sudden, very clear vison of what this gorgeous man would look like on a horse, in total control of a powerful animal, she found the idea very erotic. Of course the horse would be a black stallion … Xander would have a black leather GoT type outfit on and he would be galloping across a large open plain towards her with rugged mountains in the background. Her vivid imagination was running away with her.

"Maria?"

"Yes" she smiled.

"I said shall we go then?"

"Oh yes of course, let me just go and grab my coat and call Charles".

On the way up to her room and back again Maria gave herself a strict telling off and told herself not to be so ridiculous. She would never see this man again after a couple more days, he was only here on business; she should just savour the moment "l'instant présent" as they say in France. They left the hotel, turned right and walked around the corner past the Elie Saab boutique to where the car was waiting.

As they chatted in the car, Xander had a habit of touching her arm when he said "do you understand what I mean" if he was not sure she had understood him. She found it hard to concentrate with him so close and smelling so good.

Charles dropped them off just past the Metro line station at Trocadero and they walked around the corner. The view was stunning, this was a great viewpoint to see the Eiffel Tower from a slight distance, day or night.

They moved forward and as they went down the couple of steps Xander put his arm on her lower back in a protective way. They stopped and waited close to the balcony area and took in the amazing view of the Eiffel Tower on the other side of the Seine, the traffic driving along both banks and the many people waiting to see the lights. It was only February and they could only imagine what this area would be like in the summer, during full tourist season.

A group of students nearby had been keeping an eye on the time and started a loud 10, 9, 8, 7 countdown. Exactly on zero the tower suddenly came to life, it was covered in randomly sparkling white lights, like an enormous Christmas decoration. It was the most spectacular sight. Maria smiled like a child watching it and when she turned to Xander he had the biggest smile on his face as well. They watched transfixed as the famous tower glittered and sparkled in the night sky.

Xander put his arm around her waist and turned her to him slightly.

"Are you OK you are not too cold?" he asked, staring at her.

Maria just shook her head and held his gaze.

Xander was very tall but Maria was wearing heeled boots and so he was only about a head taller than her. They moved slightly closer together, both glanced across at the sparkling tower, then back to each other. Then Xander bent his face to hers and softly brushed her lips with his. It was the slightest touch but the electricity between them, as the lights sparkled behind them, was incredible. They stared at each other, then their lips closed together again, this time the kiss was longer and very intimate. Xander tasted so good, the chemistry between them was intense, they explored each other's mouths with their tongues, Maria ran her tongue around the back of his teeth. The desire was so strong between them it was almost palpable. They stayed like that for a few seconds longer as the kiss grew stronger, more urgent. Then, both breathing heavily, they pulled apart, staring at each other.

The Eiffel Tower had finished until the next hourly display and people were starting to disperse.

"OK I think we should go and eat" Xander breathed, looking intensely at her.

From the barely disguised desire in his dark eyes Maria got the distinct impression he was thinking perhaps more about a private dinner of champagne and strawberries, than a restaurant and she smiled at her own erotic thoughts.

"Yes let's go" she smiled at him.

Maria asked Charles to drop them not too far from the hotel, then thanked him as he went home for the night. They found a secluded restaurant in one of the streets near the Champs-Elysées and were shown to a table for two in the corner. The place was full of mostly French diners and smelled of promising culinary delights; there was soft jazz music playing and the murmur of foreign voices. The anonymity put Maria at ease, so often in NYC she would meet people she knew, but here it was almost as if they had been transported briefly into a totally different reality. Xander must feel the same, she imagined.

As they enjoyed a delicious glass of Pouilly-Fumé with their Coquilles St Jacques starter (the French name is so much more romantic than 'scallops' Maria thought), Alexander explained he ran a successful construction company in Firenze "my city that English-speaking people call Florence" and was very much hands on in the running of the company, visiting sites all day and taking care of his own emails. Maria liked his obvious 'boss who gets his hands dirty' approach and his easy manner as he joked about funny situations where people new on site had not realised he was the owner of the company.

Maria laughed and he looked serious for a minute.

"You are so beautiful when you smile, your face just lights up Maria" he said softly.

Maria looked directly into his eyes and smiled, she was watching his face with its angular nose and jawline and thinking how sensual his mouth was, his lips were fuller than you normally see in a man and she found herself thinking erotic thoughts about him, imagining how a man like that would kiss her all over.

Xander stared back and the electric frisson of excitement sparked between them again, the kind you only get with true mutual attraction. He hardly knew this woman but he knew he wanted to see a lot more of her – *much* more of her.

"But I am originally from Venezia, or Venice as you know it, my family were from a long line of fabric producers, going back generations producing velvet" he explained as he stared at her.

Maria smiled at him as he continued "although we have a French branch of the family also, my mother tells me I look like her second cousin who was from the Bordeaux region, his name was François de Lorvoire. He was suspected of working with the Germans during the second world war but in fact he was in the French resistance and saved many lives".

Maria wondered if this man could get any more romantic, that explained why he spoke a bit of French and after this Paris trip, the next time she came to Europe she wanted to visit Venice. She had seen so many pictures of the beautiful old palaces, the Grand Canal, the gondolas, St Mark's Square – and to think this man used to actually *live* there. Grew up there!

"Well Venezia is my next dream destination so you will have to tell me all about it!" she smiled at him, deliberately using the Italian name for the city.

"It would be my pleeeeasure" Xander breathed.

As he said the word 'pleasure' in his Italian accent, Maria suddenly had a vision of what Xander would look like, as he ripped off his white shirt, exposing his (she imagined) hard muscular chest and took her in his arms before kissing her passionately. Mentally shaking herself, she told herself to calm down and not be so ridiculous, she met this man just yesterday, they were on their first dinner date.

The waiter appeared to clear their starter and broke the atmosphere. Alexander's cell phone buzzed and he excused himself saying he had to take it urgently. Maria watched as he got up and moved easily, his muscular chest and shoulders barely disguised under his fitted white shirt. His suit trousers showed off his muscular butt in a subtle but very sexy way. This man knew how to dress that was for sure and he was obviously a man who looked after himself and worked out. Maria decided to try and find out exactly how old he was. She guessed early forties. The last man that had chatted her up had thought she was only 38 and he had turned out to be only 30 himself; although flattered she did not want to be attracting guys THAT young!

"I am sorry that was urgent, my son Gianni had a check-up today, he was knocked off his Vespa in Firenze last week" he said, as he walked athletically back to the table a few minutes later.

"No problem, I hope he is OK?" Maria said.

"Well he is 20 and super fit so he should recover easily" said Xander.

"20 !! " Maria exclaimed, "you don't look old enough to have a son that age!"

"Actually I have two, Gianni and his twin brother Marco" he said.

"So you have two children as well" Maria smiled, although when she said this she saw the same shadow cross Xander's handsome face, although she could not imagine why.

"Anyway, I am MUCH older than YOU, that is for sure" Xander said.

"Really, how old are you?" she asked.

"I am 48" he said, making a mock horrified face.

"Oh my goodness, so how old do you think I am?" she said.

"Well my beautiful Maria I would say you are about 42 years old".

"Really! Well I have to tell you that I have a very big birthday coming up fairly soon" Maria said, feigning shock.

"Oh no, no no, I am so sorry, so so sorry, mi dispiace Maria, so you are 39" he looked truly horrified "what can I say to make this up to you, I am such an idiot, I am no good at guessing age" he gazed at her with a mortified expression.

Maria looked at his stunningly handsome face, now so downcast and worried that he had really put his foot in it. She took a sip of wine, and leaned in across the small table, he did the same, inwardly delighted that she did not seem too offended.

"Xander" she whispered.

"Maria" he leaned closer.

They were centimetres apart and she could smell his maleness, his perfume and the wine on his breath. Xander could sense her like he had never sensed another woman before.

"I need to tell you something" she breathed "come closer".

Xander could not help himself, he felt the electricity as surely as she must be feeling it, and in the dimly lit corner at their table for two, he leaned just a bit closer and his sensual lips brushed hers for the second time that evening. The electricity was so strong Maria thought afterwards that surely a physical spark must have shot between them.

"Please forgive me" Xander surprised himself at how breathless he was after such a fleeting kiss.

"Xander"

"Yes Maria"

Their lips were still so close she could feel his breath.

"I am 48 years old".

Maria had never seen a smile so wide appear so fast on anyone's face!

"But no no no you are joking" but he carried on smiling "you are trying to make me feel better".

"I promise you it's true but thank you for thinking I am only 42" "or even 39!" she joked.

The waiter appeared with their main course at that moment. Alexander had chosen his favourite Italian dish spaghetti alle vongole and Maria had sea bass with a delicate red thai sauce.

"Bon appétit" and the waiter melted away.

Xander was still in shock, and unbelievably relieved he had been so wrong. Yet he could still not believe Maria was the same age he was, as she looked so young, so fit, so sexy. A couple of his female employees were about 50 and they looked absolutely nothing like Maria! Worse, his ex-wife was the *same* age, 48, and although beautiful in her youth, now looked at least five years older!

Maria looked at him and said simply "age is just a number Xander".

He just stared at her.

"Some people are born old, others stay forever young, it all depends on your spirit and your way of thinking" she continued and then she smiled "plus I do work hard in the gym to keep my butt in shape!!"

Xander could think of several answers to that but he kept his private thoughts to himself. He had seen how she looked in running gear and in jeans, and in her dress tonight her figure was stunning, very athletically fit but sexy at the same time. He found himself wondering what underwear she was wearing ... and what her skin would feel like, smell like ... his mind wandered.

"Xander?"

"Yes soorrrry"

"I asked if you like working out in the gym"

"Oh yes yes" Xander collected himself "at my company headquarters in Firenze I built a gym with sauna, jacuzzi and also a massage jet therapy pool. It is free for all my staff including the guys out on the construction sites. Healthy workers are happy workers! We also have a juice bar, we are very thinking forwards is that 'ow you say it?"

"Forward thinking" she smiled, Maria was impressed at this, and also found it sweet that occasionally he did not know the correct expression in English for something.

The rest of the meal passed very quickly, they talked about so many things and lost track of time. Neither of them felt as if it was the first time they had had dinner, it felt as if they had known each other so much longer. Maria told Xander about her two beautiful daughters, Luisa and Carla, who were 16 and 18 and expecting plenty of presents from the fashion capital of the world! They laughed and joked. When Maria mentioned how great it was having grown up children who you could leave in charge of the house, and left you free to enjoy life, the same shadow crossed his face as earlier in the evening. Maria was vaguely confused but didn't comment. They didn't kiss again but the looks that passed between them betrayed their desire that both were trying to control. By the time they had finished coffee it was late. Xander helped Maria with her coat and brushed her arm sensually as he did so. Maria felt a jolt of desire run through her core to her deep well of femininity and felt a twitch from her secret place ... her body clearly did not agree with her decision to avoid men. Xander paid and they went outside. Charles and the car were nowhere to be seen so Maria called him.

"He will be here in five minutes" she said as the light Parisian rain started up again.

"Let's take shelter here in the entrance to a boutique" said Xander.

They stood close together listening to the rain on the sidewalk and the splashing of the traffic through the wet roads. Xander placed his hand on her waist and said.

"Maria I really enjoyed dinner tonight".

At his touch she looked up at his handsome face and they held each other's gaze for a long time.

Xander turned to take her in his arms. As he pulled her closer Maria felt electricity shoot through her once again and from the look on his face, he felt it too.

"Maria you are so beautiful" he whispered, leaning towards her … Maria offered her mouth to his and his sensual lips touched hers lightly then more urgently as they kissed and kissed. Xander pulled her strongly to him so that she could feel his muscular chest and his hardness in his trousers. Although they were both fully clothed and wearing coats she sensed this Italian was very well endowed, every part of him felt hard. Neither of them wanted the kiss to stop. At the sound of the approaching car they pulled away from each other while still holding eye contact, trying to control their breathing.

"Bonsoir" said Charles as he got out to open the car door for them "are you ready to return to the hotel?"

They got into the car and Zeus greeted them enthusiastically from the trunk, having been taken for a walk by Charles who fortunately was a real dog lover. Xander explained he had brought the dog with him to Paris as he had travelled by car from Italy, visiting clients on the way in Genoa, Aix-en-Provence and Lyon. As he was explaining he reached over to take Maria's hand and at his touch she felt desire stir within her again; this man had such an effect on her she was quite shocked at herself. The few guys she had dated in the last couple of years had been attractive and she had had more than a few hot dates, but nothing close to this intense feeling she had with Xander.

"My boys are with their mama this week and I don't like to leave him for too long if I can help it, he likes to be with me" Xander explained.

Maria wondered if this gorgeous guy could get any cuter – he was even a dog lover. The same race of dog she loved too! She squeezed his hand lightly as she looked at his even, lightly tanned skin, long elegant fingers with nicely manicured fingernails, the hint of dark hair on his arms … she found herself imagining his muscular chest and touching the hair on his torso. She wondered if he could read her thoughts on her face.

"Would you like to have a drink in the hotel bar before the night ends?" he asked her, staring at her with his intense dark brown eyes.

Maria, despite her resolution to avoid men this trip, really did not want this evening to end. And, she told herself, he will only be here for another few days, I am here for a week, so why not? What could possibly happen in a couple of days … she was quite safe, she should enjoy the present moment.

"Yes let's do that" she agreed, looking into his eyes.

They got back to the hotel at nearly midnight and ordered drinks; they sat in the bar in a corner on one of the sumptuous sofas. They talked about travel, Maria's life in NYC, Venice, Xander's business, his mysterious French distant cousin François de Lorvoire (what a dashing name Maria thought), her Argentinian/Italian ancestry, so many things, the time flew by.

"OK I really have to get to bed" Maria smiled.

"Me also" said Xander in his delicious Italian accent "let me walk you to your suite".

They left the bar and Xander put his hand lightly on her shoulder in a protective gesture as they walked together to the elevator. There was nobody about that late so the elevator opened immediately. They walked in and Xander turned to Maria.

"Thank you for a really enjoyable evening Maria" he was very close to her.

"It's been lovely" Maria breathed, moving imperceptibly closer to him.

Xander suddenly put his hands on her hips firmly pushing her back against the side of the elevator, Maria's heart was already beating wildly. He leant down and their lips met again, softly at first but very quickly much more strongly than before. The kiss was passionate, his mouth crushing hers with his desire, she was pinned against the elevator. Maria put her hands inside his jacket as he kissed her and felt his muscular back through his shirt. The smell of his perfume was affecting her senses and she felt sheer electric desire for him.

As the elevator started moving, he pushed hard against her, kissing her passionately, Maria could feel his large male hardness in his trousers again and his unmistakeable desire. His mouth tasted so good, the chemistry between them was incredible. She pulled his shirt loose from his trousers and ran her hands up his back. There was not an inch of fat on this guy, he was in amazing shape; his back was very muscled and his skin was beautifully smooth. She moved her hands down and felt his rounded, tight butt through his trousers. She pulled his hips towards her, the desire running through her body. At the touch of her hands Xander's tongue grew even more urgent, their tongues were exploring each other, their bodies pressed together … it seemed as if time had stopped. The elevator came to a halt, they had arrived at Maria's suite. They quickly pulled apart as the doors opened, but nobody was there.

At her door they kissed passionately again, their bodies melting into one another with the desire neither could control. Maria had already decided though, that there was no way she was sleeping with him after one date, although she wanted to.

The kiss got slower, more intimate if that was possible and finally their tongues were just teasing each other lightly. They pulled apart finally, holding eye contact and not saying anything.

Alexander did not suggest a nightcap or anything further, he sensed that this was the end of the evening. Although since he had been single, for the last few years, he had had no problem picking up girls and sleeping with them very quickly, he did not want to do that with Maria. He knew she wanted him and from recent experience he knew he was very attractive to women. He had gone a bit crazy after he divorced. Sex with his wife after 23 years together had become routine and boring, with nothing to spice it up. He had known he was not alone in this situation and many couples just stayed together through habit, for the kids, because they didn't want to divorce, because they didn't want to lose money etc, etc, all the usual reasons.

He had finally left three years previously, not for another woman but because he had had "un sesto senso" a sixth sense pushing him into change. He had felt optimistic for the future and that he was destined for something in his life beyond what he had experienced for the last 23 years, although he did not yet know what. He had kept imagining himself travelling, but not with his wife. Although 23 years was a long time (the friends that tell you not to "throw away nearly a quarter of a century") the thought of another potentially 30 or 40 years of the same "acceptable and conventional" life just ate away at him. The divorce had not been easy but the boys had taken it well, they had not seemed overly surprised. They had been through a wild patch aged around 15-16 and luckily had calmed down by the time he left their mother. His ex had not found anyone else that he knew of, but she communicated with him if necessary, with no bad feeling. How long that would go on for he was not sure, he thought darkly, thinking of a conversation he would soon be having with her. In any case he always treated her with respect, as the mother of his kids. The boys were adults, so they did not have the problems some of his friends had had, who divorced when their kids were small.

"Maria, I have meetings all day tomorrow but would you like to have dinner tomorrow night?" asked Xander, slightly breathless despite his efforts to remain aloof.

The fact that "tomorrow" was February 14 and Saint Valentine's Day was not lost on Maria and she smiled.

"Yes I would like that very much Xander" she replied.

Inwardly Xander was delighted. This American lady had had a real effect on him and he was not entirely sure he was enjoying being totally taken over by his feelings, although he desperately wanted to see her again as soon as possible. The other women he had met since his divorce, some of them had been really hot, but he had seen them once or twice and moved on, as they seemed to get attached to him way too quickly. He never got attached. He was absolutely not ready for anything serious with someone. With work and a personal issue that had come up recently he had waaay too much going on his life already.

"OK that's great. Maybe we can meet in the bar first, can I take your number and I will message you, in case one of my meetings is late".

She gave him her cell phone number and they exchanged one last long slow kiss, their tongues exploring each other's mouths in a slow sensuous embrace and it was as if time would stand still for however long they wished, their bodies pressed against each other. She could feel Xander's impressive hardness again through his trousers and his male scent was driving her wild. In her mind she could already imagine what this unbelievably sexy man would look like naked ... they eventually pulled apart and Maria slipped inside her room as Xander went back to his suite.

Maria was not at all tired, in spite of it being very late and being jet lagged (and her morning run, she remembered!) she felt a lot of energy coursing through her. She decided to take a long shower in the sumptuous bathroom to try and calm her racing heart down, then journal a little. She liked to note down ideas and feelings in her journal. Not like a diary, more like an expression of her inner being. She found herself being slightly sad at the thought of Xander only being in Paris for a few more days.

She took off her dress and slipped out of her black lacy underwear and hold ups. She had a flash of an erotic idea and decided to wear her garter belt with stockings tomorrow instead of holdups. They made her feel sexier and she felt an urge to wear them. Of course over here in Europe English people called them "suspenders" Maria thought with a smile. The French had a much prettier word for them and called them "portes-jarretelles". Since her separation Maria had accumulated quite a number of erotic outfits, garter belts and heels to match. Sex with her husband had become quite boring, now she felt as if she had a new lease of life, approaching her 50th birthday next year, and she intended to make the most of life in all areas.

As the hot water and strong jets massaged her body she wondered if Xander was doing the same in his shower. She imagined him there with her, caressing her body with his strong hands. As she soaped herself and felt the water running over herself, she caressed her pussy, her fingers playing with her nub, it did not take long to bring herself to a quivering climax, alone under the hot water.

That night she dreamt of Paris, but a centuries-older Paris, there was cannon and musket fire and she was a lady in a tight-bodiced, exquisite velvet gown, running through the smoke away from one of the revolutionists, who caught her and pinned her against a wall. Except then he turned into Xander and he was rescuing her, not trying to attack her, and pressing his hard, muscular body against her, he held her against the mediaeval wall, kissing her passionately.

▲▲▲

CHAPTER FOUR

▲

SAINT VALENTINE'S DAY

February 14

Maria woke up very early, her thoughts immediately turning to the sexy Italian and their kiss the night before. She lay in bed for a moment, thinking about their dinner date tonight and felt a jolt of excitement in her stomach at the thought of seeing him again. Honestly Maria, she thought to herself, what are you like! This was supposed to be a relaxing week of museums and spa treatments, safely away from any guys! She sighed, smiling naughtily to herself and checked her cell for messages that had come in from NYC when she was already sleeping last night. She was looking forward to a bit of shopping in Paris later that morning that she had planned. She had an appointment in the spa for a body scrub/massage booked for 8.30am and she wanted to get a short run in first, in the hotel gym. Although she was working out she still put on concealer, eyeliner and waterproof mascara.   As she did so she could understand why people called her vain, but at approaching fifty a small amount of make-up makes such a big difference, both visually and mentally. Anyway, she thought to herself, I can do what the hell I like, who cares if I am going to the gym! She put on her shorts, t-shirt and her running shoes and made her way down.

The gym in the hotel was gorgeous, so many machines and lovely piles of white towels for the guests to use. At this hour the gym was empty. She went straight to a treadmill and entered 5.5km. She started running and after 500m pushed the pace up a bit and settled in for a steady 25 minute 5km run. She had her running playlist in her ears and happily zoned out into a rhythm.

She didn't realise towards the end of her run that she had an admiring spectator… Alexander Sabatini had come to the gym as he liked to exercise early morning, particularly before business meetings. It kept him sharp. As he entered the gym, in a black vest and shorts which showed off his muscular physique, he noticed Maria immediately, and stopped to watch her. She was clearly in a world of her own, concentrating on her sport. He watched her running smoothly then push up the pace to a fast sprint for the final couple of minutes of her run. He admired her long legs, glad that nobody else was exercising at this hour and he could watch her without looking like some weirdo stalker. As she slowed down then stopped, she reached for her towel and dried her face, happily sweaty. She stepped off the machine backwards and did a couple of slow calf stretches, still not aware that Xander was watching. He admired her very fit behind as she stretched her legs. As she moved sideways slightly to hold on to the handrail and stretch her quads she noticed him there.

"Xander" she exclaimed "good morning, you are up as early as me! How long have you been here?"

"I just arrived" Xander said, although she had the distinct impression that he had been there more than a few minutes and smiled to herself at the thought of him watching her.

"Good run?" he asked, smiling at her.

Maria looked at his honed body dressed in sportswear and his lightly tanned skin. She felt a rush of desire run through her body.

"Great thanks, I love to run" she smiled "but I can't chat I have to go, I have a full body massage booked, I hope you have a good workout".

She knew that mentioning her body massage would put ideas into Xander's head and she was not wrong. He had a very clear mental image of what she would feel like, under his hands, as he gave her a sensual massage with oils …

"OK have a good morning, and I'll see you later" he smiled "about 8pm is OK for you?"

"Perfect" said Maria, looking at him and once again feeling herself drawn into his beautiful deep brown eyes with their dark lashes. Her eyes moved down, taking in his muscular arms and shoulders, as he smiled at her. He was absolutely gorgeous.

"See you later" he said, staring intently at her and touching her arm gently as he moved into the gym.

She quickly showered off in the luxurious changing room in the gym as she didn't want to arrive sweaty for her spa appointment.

In the spa she lay very chilled out having her treatment, which was the most relaxing she had ever had. The products smelt heavenly. Maria did not believe you could spend too much on beauty products and beauty treatments, this was utter bliss. She had a full body scrub treatment with a clay product, followed by a massage with oils. After her workout this morning it was perfect, and she felt any jetlag and muscle tension release. The whole experience was just over an hour and she floated back to her room to get ready for the day ahead.

When she returned to her suite, she found room service arriving to deliver her full English breakfast with toast and coffee. She gulped down the orange juice and then ate hungrily. The presentation of the food at this hotel was second to none and it was absolutely delicious.

She showered, then straightened her hair, before applying full make-up, ready for the day ahead. She always looked nice, but she also knew that the French were a bit disdainful of American and English women, with regard to the effort they put into their appearance, so she took time to look good. She was wearing jeans, sneakers, a white sweatshirt and a hooded waterproof jacket as it looked as if the light Parisian rain was threatening again.

She headed left out of the hotel and straight to the Champs-Elysées. She looked up to her left and admired the Arc de Triomphe as she crossed the wide avenue and went straight to Sephora, where she spent a girly half hour trying perfumes, beauty products and make up. She practised her French on some of the sales staff, who were pleased to meet an American who was attempting to speak their language. Maria realised though, that she needed to work on her language skills a little! She bought some of the latest Dior makeup and some things for her girls. From there she went to the huge Adidas store and treated herself to some more gymwear.

She headed further down the avenue and found a Zadig and Voltaire boutique where she tried on various outfits. The fit of their clothes was always perfect for her and she ended up buying several pairs of jeans, some light jumpers, tops and two pairs of cowboy style boots. She loved their designs as they were slightly edgy but still classic, she was always very careful (at her age she smiled) not to be too logo covered or too young looking. It was a balance between classic and still sexy as opposed to frumpy. Her daughters were very good at helping her choose clothes and would always tell her the blunt truth "mom that's way too young for you" if necessary. She was "allowed" quirky coloured boots and shoes but nothing else too overly loud, they always told her. They were so funny. She smiled at the thought of her girls and promised them in her head that they would all come to Paris very soon, together. She suddenly thought of that future trip, which was highly unlikely to include bumping into a handsome Italian called Xander in the lobby on arrival, and she felt oddly sad. Then she caught herself, told herself not to be so silly, and arranged with the sales girl for her purchases to be delivered back to the hotel that morning.

She left the boutique and headed to the classically beautiful streets behind the Champs-Elysées. She walked through to the Palais de l'Elysée in the 8th arrondissement which was built in 1722 but since 1848 had been the seat of the French government. Its address was so romantic she thought, 55 rue du Faubourg Saint-Honoré. All the architecture in this area was stunning and she could sense the ancient history in this beautiful city.

From there she walked back through towards Place Vendôme, stopping at a beautiful old wine shop to buy a bottle of Moët & Chandon pink, or rosé impérial, champagne. She could probably have ordered it from room service but there was something about spending time in these ancient streets and shops and choosing your own from the selection of wines from all the famous vineyards in France. She hoped she might be sharing it with Xander later, as it was fairly clear after their dinner last night where things were headed. But even if not, she intended to toast to new beginnings.

Apart from the exquisite taste of the French champagnes, Maria loved the history and had read up on lots of things before her visit. She knew the champagne House of Moët & Chandon had been founded by Claude Moët in 1743. King Louis XV, with his taste for sparkling wine, had made champagnes fashionable. Claude Moët was the first winemaker to exclusively produce sparkling wine and she knew the House also have a royal warrant to supply champagne to the English royal family. Maria had also found out, as nobody ever seems to be sure, that Moët is pronounced "mo-wett" as Claude had Dutch origins. His name was never pronounced "mo-way", with a French accent, they always pronounced the "t". Moët became the famous Moët & Chandon in 1833 when Pierre-Gabriel Chandon joined the House as a partner to Jean-Remy Moët, the grandson of Claude. Another gem Maria had discovered before leaving NYC was that apparently the French love of "sabring", or dramatically slicing the glass top directly off the champagne bottle with a sword or sabre, was started by Napoleon to celebrate winning battles. Some party trick, Maria thought with a smile.

One day, maybe with her girls, she wanted to actually go to the vineyard and have a tour of Moët & Chandon to see the process and visit the "cave" or wine cellars. It looked fascinating and the region of Champagne looked so beautiful in pictures. As Maria put her bottle of Moët in her backpack she smiled to herself as she imagined herself back in NYC, adding the popped cork, marked with the date it was opened and the occasion, to her collection of "special occasion" corks. She had started it a while back, as a way of collecting "toast to" memories all in one place, and she had a sudden rush of desire for what she anticipated might happen tonight (not that she was going to write *that* on the cork she giggled to herself). Her mind wandered to the night before, her final goodnight kiss with Xander. She congratulated herself on not sleeping with him the very first evening, as this was clearly a very time limited encounter, but the desire and attraction between them was not only undeniable, it was unstoppable, and she felt totally ready for whatever tonight might bring.

She felt lighter and happier than she had for years, as she continued wandering alone through the streets, taking photos of picturesque street views and of Place Vendôme before buying an intricate gold and peridot bracelet in Van Cleef & Arpels. She WhatsApped lots of photos to her girls and her friends, they would still be asleep of course as it was still very early morning in NYC.

She decided to do some people-watching over lunchtime and found a café on the corner of two classic streets. She sat down outside but near the café wall, thankful the terrace heaters were doing a good job of keeping the air warm under the awning. It was a busy area and she admired the way people were dressed as they passed by, most on their way to work lunches. She didn't want to eat too much this evening on their date, she never ate a large amount at night in any case, but she had been in the gym so she decided to order a typical French snack, a Croque-Monsieur, with a large plate of chips and salad. It was basically a glorified ham and cheese toasted sandwich, but so delicious. She was just adoring having so much time to herself, in her "previous" life that had just never happened! She ordered a coffee and a "coeur coulant au chocolat" which turned out to be mini chocolate cake with a runny centre. It was absolutely awesome. *"Lucky I am only here for a week"* Maria thought to herself, she would be the size of a horse if she stayed any longer. She went into the ornate old café and paid the bartender, then headed in the direction of the Louvre. This time she was going to go in and visit the Egyptian section for a couple of hours.

She arrived after a couple of streets at the rue de Rivoli, crossed over, and entered the Louvre by way of the eastern entrance which led down through the shopping centre hidden beneath the courtyard. She passed the original mediaeval foundations of the ancient castle, stopped for a moment to soak in the ancient vibe of the place, then carried on to the entrance gates to the museum. She looked up at the huge glass pyramid which was now above her and admired the design of it, it was truly beautiful.

As she made her way to the department of Egyptian antiquities, she realised you could easily get lost in the Louvre. She knew it was the world's largest museum, but it really was absolutely massive! She spent a happy couple of hours admiring the statues and columns with their ornate hieroglyphics, followed by the Greek, Etruscan and Roman displays and finished in the Islamic Art department.

It was getting late in the afternoon and she decided to make her way back to the hotel. She walked back through the Tuileries Garden and when she reached the Place de la Concorde, just on a whim, she decided to get one of the bicycle taxis they had seen yesterday back to the Champs-Elysées. She found one, paid the "driver" who was a very friendly student who earned extra money by cycling tourists around the area, and they set off. It was so much fun, he pedalled impressively fast, the bike bobbed slightly perilously around the cobbled roundabout amongst all the traffic, then they headed up the Champs-Elysées.

"Where you want to stop?" the driver asked her and she got him to drop her off just opposite the avenue George V "merci beaucoup" she smiled at him and made her way across the Champs-Elysées and down to the hotel.

It was now late morning in NYC so she decided to call her girls and find out how they were doing. Of course the girls asked her what she had been doing, so she told them all about the places she had seen. But then came the obvious question …

"Any attractive guys Mom?" they asked. "France must be full of romantic men isn't it?"

"Well actually I am having dinner with someone tonight" she admitted.

"Whaaaaat, are you serious" Luisa exclaimed "who, what's he like, where did you meet him?!!"

"Calm down he is just another guest in this hotel and actually he is Italian not French!"

"Oooooh" came the joint reply.

"And guess what, he has a dog just like Bella, here in the hotel!" she told them.

"No way" they said, intrigued to find out there was a Great Dane like theirs staying in Paris.

They chatted for a bit longer, Maria heading them off the subject before they could ask too many questions. She then called her friend Anna but no reply, Anna was an interior designer and was probably working so Maria left a message. Her next call was to Luke, a handsome gay friend of theirs, he was a personal trainer, but she got his voicemail. Luke was the sort of guy that when women found out he was gay the first comment was always a smiling "what a waste!" as he was seriously gorgeous and very muscular. So far he had not been lucky in love but he had been hinting lately that things might be changing. Luke was an amazing cook and his place had been the venue for many fun evenings.

She then called Lisette who answered immediately. Lisette worked in film set design part time and also at Pier 59. She was to come to France herself quite soon on a two-week set design project near Marseille. She was a tall vivacious blonde who always seemed to pick the bad boys and was yet again single. It was Lisette who had introduced Maria to the ex-professional basketballer player Maria had dated briefly, Lisette had got his number during a photo shoot she had organised and told him she had a friend who might like to meet him. Lisette was not shy in match making. Maria smiled to herself as she remembered how the 6'9" basketballer had used to pick her up like she was a Barbie doll and make love to her standing up. He had had a dream physique but neither of them had been ready for a relationship and after a few very hot months it eventually fizzled out. Lisette usually worked late hours, so she was home this morning in NYC. Maria briefly explained what had happened with Xander and braced herself for an interrogation.

"WTF!!!" Lisette screeched "Maria you told me you were off dudes, going to Europe to 'find yourself' blah blah ... OMG I cannot believe this, tell me all about him RIGHT NOW!! Have you kissed him?" Lisette was immediately totally hyper.

"Calm down Lise" Maria laughed "and errrrm yes I have".

Screams down the line from NYC ...

"OMGGGGGG" Lisette was beside herself "so what does he look like?"

Maria described Xander, his long dark hair, his angular face, his muscular shoulders, his tanned skin, his full lips and kissing ability.

"OMGGG you have found an Italian Stallion!!" Lise squealed "has he got a brother??"

Maria could not stop laughing as she said she didn't know, but she would try and find out tonight.

"Ohhh he sounds amazing, you MUST call me tomorrow to tell me how dinner *and anything else* goes, OK" Lise said "oh and if he does have a brother who is single you can get his number" she giggled loudly "I need to meet a real man. You know that creepy guy who came to the shoot last week I told you about? The one who was like 5'5". He wanted my number. They fall for me all the time and think I feel the same OMG"

"Lise you will meet the right guy I know" Maria said. She had the same problem with guys, they tended to fall in love after a couple of lunch dates and think she felt the same. Single guys around 50 tend to fall into two camps: either they have been left by their wives and get attached WAY too quickly as they don't want to be alone, or, newly single after 20-25 years in a sexless marriage they are too busy playing the field. It was extremely complicated finding one who was over his break-up, happily independent and actually looking for something serious. That was why, Maria reminded herself, she was concentrating on herself and her future and NOT getting involved with anyone.

After telling her a bit about Paris and what she had done so far, Maria promised she would call Lise tomorrow.

**

Maria took a long time getting ready for their second dinner date. She showered then re-straightened her hair as it was naturally very curly and with the damp weather it was trying to re-curl. Then she carefully applied full makeup, taking care to get a flawless base finish and just the right amount of blush and highlight. For her eyes she applied slightly darker brown shades of eyeshadow and tightlined her eyes in waterproof Chanel black eyeliner which accentuated their blue colour, before applying mascara. She outlined her lips and applied a pretty Dior lipstick. She examined her face in the mirror, pleased with the effect, she was very slightly lined but she made the most of her features, drawing attention away from any flaws. She knew she looked younger than her years but at the same time did not want to look 25. Getting the right balance with clothes and makeup as you got older was tricky that was for sure.

**

Xander had taken Zeus out for a walk and was back in his suite, trying to decide whether to wear a white shirt or a black one *cosa stai pensando, sei pazzo?* he thought to himself, are you crazy? He had just showered and was in his bedroom wearing only a white towel around his waist. He was annoyed with himself at how strongly Maria had affected him. *Just put on the black shirt* he told himself. As he buttoned his shirt, leaving the top two buttons open to reveal a hint of his muscular chest, he told himself to just enjoy the moment. Then, he needed to concentrate on returning to Italy, his upcoming construction projects and the most recent issue that had just come up which he needed to deal with, he thought, with a pang of anxiety. He needed to get a bit more focused on that and less on the beautiful American woman he only met two days ago.

**

Maria had decided on a classic fitted black dress for this evening. She clipped her stockings onto her garter belt, then slipped on her panties and bra and admired herself in the large full-length mirror. She worked hard to look this good and always made time to appreciate her physical appearance. She put on her black stiletto heels and posed in front of the mirror, taking sexy selfies. She knew she looked good. She would keep these pictures to look at when she was home and remembering her much-more-exciting-than-anticipated week in Paris! She took some from the front, then from the side, making sure her booty was shown off to full perfection and her legs looked as long as possible. Then she turned around and took some rear-view pictures in the mirror before cropping them down. "Maria you are damn hot" she told herself, smiling naughtily as she looked at one she had taken, leaning forward in her garter belt, her legs looking super long in the heels and with one hand sexily on her butt as she tilted slightly to one side.

She put on her dress, gave her make-up one last touch up and left her suite.

Maria surprised herself at being slightly nervous as she went down in the elevator and made her way to the bar.

Xander saw her approaching and caught his breath, she looked stunning, again. There was nothing this lady could not wear without looking sexy, he thought. Running gear, jeans, classy dresses … he took a deep breath before standing and greeting her.

"You look stunning Maria, really beautiful this evening" he murmured as he kissed her cheek, putting his hands on her upper arms in a way as if to say "this woman is taken" in case any of the several admiring men in the bar had any doubt.

Just looking at Xander caused Maria's heart to leap in her chest, but as he ordered champagne and they settled into chatting and laughing together, any nerves just disappeared; they quickly became very relaxed together, as they had been the day before. Except tonight they were both acutely aware that they both wanted the evening to go further than the previous date. As they were talking, both found that they would be in the middle of a sentence and then just stop, forgetting what they were going to say next, put off by the electric attraction already buzzing between them. Then, gazing at each other with undisguised desire in their eyes, they would laugh it off, knowing the feeling was mutual. Xander put his hand on her knee as they chatted and left it there; Maria could smell his Dior Sauvage and his maleness every time he leant in to speak to her. It was driving her crazy but she tried not to show how affected she was by him.

"So do you have a picture of your sons?" Maria asked Xander.

"Oh yes" he smiled.

He got out his phone and showed her a picture of the two boys together and she immediately exclaimed "wow Xander they are gorgeous boys!"

The twins were stunning and actually looked quite like the handsome Matteo Bocelli. They had their father's good looks but with a younger, less worldly appearance. Sometimes Xander had a curious, slightly haunted look on his gorgeous face. They were good looking boys and Maria laughed to herself at what her daughters would think of them.

"Xander who is that in the picture?" Maria asked, pointing at two men and a woman with the twins in one photo.

"Those are my brothers and sister" Xander smiled widely "Cristofano, Antonio and Chiara, they are all younger than me. Antonio and Cristo live in Firenze, Chiara lives in Roma".

Maria was already mentally picturing Lisette's reaction to the very good looking brothers and she smiled, she had to ask the question, some detective work just for Lise :

"Oh so are they all married?" she asked ...

"Chiara is the youngest, she is 38 and married with three daughters and like I said they live in Rome" Xander said "Antonio is married but I am not sure what is happening, he does not seem happy. He has a boy and a girl. Cristo has two boys, a bit younger than Gianni and Marco". Antonio is a chef, he has a successful restaurant in Firenze. He runs, he has run a lot of marathons, he is 40. Cristo is 43 and single, he just got divorced. He runs three gyms in the city, he has a really good business".

This news made Maria smile, at the thought of the reaction from NYC, even though these guys were living on a different continent!

Lise was younger than Maria at 44 but her kids were the same ages as Maria's. Lise liked her men younger, she was really beautiful, always dating models but it never lasted.

"And do you have a picture of your daughters Maria?" Xander asked.

Maria showed him a picture of Luisa and Carla and he was very impressed, telling her how pretty they both were. Luisa had blue eyes with very long, blonde hair and Carla had darker hair and greeny-blue eyes. Both girls were very sporty. Maria explained how they both played golf and basketball. They all liked to go to the Knicks games in Madison Square Garden as often as possible.

"Oh Gianni and Marco play basketball also, they are pretty tall" Xander smiled "but they love football the best!"

Maria told Xander she had two brothers but no sisters. Xander thought it was funny that her brothers also had Italian names, Paolo and Giorgio.

"So my father's family was ancestrally from northern Italy, he was a huge fan of the Riva family, their history and the boats" Maria explained "I just adore the sea, swimming and sailing" she explained.

"Yes, me too I love the sea" he said and of course he knew exactly what she was talking about. He had gone to the Salone Nautico Venezia last year, the boat show in Venice, and knew all about the Riva yachting dynasty. The company had been started further north of Florence in Sarnico in the Italian lakes. Lake Iseo was where Pietro Riva had started the famous boatbuilding company in 1842. Xander also loved swimming and had done plenty of swim training over the years to complement his gym work. No wonder she was so fit, he thought, his mind wandering to what might happen later that night …

He touched her arm as he asked her "shall we go to eat now?"

Maria looked into his eyes and they held eye contact for a long time, as he slid his hand down her arm and clasped her hand in both of his.

"What would you like to eat Maria?" he gazed at her intently.

The touch of his hand made her quiver "I am not sure" she smiled "shall we get Charles to drive us and we can stop if we see a nice restaurant we like the look of?"

Xander reached forward, still holding her hand and kissed her cheek lightly as he whispered, "that sounds perfect", rolling the 'r' in his sexy Italian accent.

Maria called Charles and the car arrived a few minutes later.

They set off and Charles gave them a bit of a guided tour around Paris after dark, driving around streets that Maria had not seen before, all of which were so classically beautiful. All of the monuments and a lot of the galleries were illuminated. Xander had not stopped holding her hand since they got into the car and at his touch she felt herself melting inside at the thought of what might happen later, what she hoped would happen later. As he leaned over to look at something Charles was pointing out on Maria's side, Xander put his hand on her thigh. He caught his breath as he felt what she was wearing under her dress. He looked at her and felt himself stiffen just at the thought of what she would look like minus her dress.

They passed a cosy looking brasserie and asked Charles to stop.

They chatted easily with each other over a dinner of coq au vin with exquisite tiny roasted potatoes. For dessert they had the most delicious rich but light creation based on the traditional mille-feuilles which consisted of multiple layers of wafer-thin sweet puff pastry, interspersed with cream and strawberries. It was sheer seduction in a dessert and as Xander watched her licking the cream off her lips his thoughts were already ahead of him … as he thought of what he would like to do to her, he felt the familiar stirring in his trousers as they finished eating.

As they waited for Charles to come and pick them up, they once again took shelter in the doorway of a boutique. Xander pulled Maria to him, held her close and kissed her passionately. As he pressed his body against his and held her firmly, she could feel his hardness and she felt herself twitch in anticipation.

▲▲▲

CHAPTER FIVE

▲

PARISIAN NIGHT

February 14

"What has Zeus been doing today?" Maria asked with a smile as they returned from dinner.

Xander told her that after the gym he had taken him for his walk in the Bois de Boulogne this morning, then he had spent most of the afternoon in the hotel room. Maria knew that the huge dogs were actually very easy to travel with as they spent most of their time sleeping.

"But right now Maria I need to take him out, if you would like to come with me?"

He went and retrieved Zeus from his suite and together they walked him around the block, before returning to the hotel. They made a very handsome couple which, together with the impressive dog they had with them, attracted stares from people in the street.

Neither noticed the attention they were getting however, as they obliviously chatted together, constantly exchanging glances. Every time Maria looked at Xander she got an electric jolt of desire that caught her breath and travelled down through her belly, she was still in awe at the reaction she had to this man's animal magnetism, just looking at him she could feel her nub pulsating in her black lace panties. As she walked she could feel her garter clips moving sexily against her legs.

As they returned to the hotel Xander did not suggest drinks in the hotel bar, as he had the previous night.

"Can I drop Zeus then walk you to your suite Maria?" he said as they crossed the lobby, the dark desire unmistakeable in his eyes.

"Of course" she stared back at him, not quite able to control her breathing, her stomach had butterflies of anticipation.

They got into the elevator and as soon as the doors closed Xander encircled her with his arms and once again pushed her hard against the side as the elevator started to move. They kissed passionately again, Xander's hands were exploring her neck, her breasts through her dress, his breathing was ragged and she could feel his excitement hard in his trousers. Maria ran her hands through his long black hair, over his shoulders and then ran her hands down his back. She could feel the muscles either side of his spine and as he pushed his body against her she felt her secret place becoming moist as her clit twitched in anticipation. Neither of them was in any doubt what was about to happen tonight, but both were also wanting to savour the moment.

As the elevator opened, they stepped out and headed to his suite where he settled Zeus back onto his bed and gave him a drink of water.

Xander returned to Maria who was waiting outside and together they walked to Maria's suite.

"So would you like to come in for a drink?" she turned to ask Xander, as she looked at his intensely masculine face, full of desire he was not trying to hide.

"Si certo Maria" Xander breathed.

He stroked her hair as she opened the door and placed his hand on her lower back as they entered the suite.

"Please have a seat" she gestured to the sofa.

Xander sat down and watched her while Maria placed two champagne glasses on the coffee table and retrieved the bottle of pink Moët & Chandon she had bought earlier, from the fridge. She put it in the ice bucket and brought it to the table. As she walked she was intensely aware of her "portes jarretelles" she was wearing moving under her dress, she felt feminine and sexy.

"Would you like to do the honours?" she asked him, handing him the bottle.

Xander had no idea what "the honours" meant but it was clear what she wanted him to do; he popped opened the bottle and poured it expertly into the two glasses. Xander stood and they each picked up a glass and for a long time just stared at each other. Neither of them felt that they had only known each other for just two days and neither wanted to remember that Xander would be driving back to Italy in two days' time.

"To unexpected pleasurable encounters?" Xander suggested as a toast, gazing at her intensely.

"To Paris and very unexpected experiences!" Maria said, looking into his eyes.

They took a sip of the delicious champagne, keeping eye contact. Then Xander took her glass and put it down on the table, and placed his glass with it after he took a sip of champagne ... he drew her to him and kissed her gently, and as he did so she felt the cold champagne trickle into her mouth, from his, it was the most erotic sensation. They kissed for a long time, pressed tightly together, their bodies hungry with desire, then Xander's hands moved to the zip on the back of her dress ... he unzipped it and Maria told him to go and sit on the sofa.

He watched as Maria let the black dress fall to the ground and even though he was expecting her to have a sensational body, he caught his breath. He could seriously not believe her age, she had a body of a 40 year old woman, and a fit one at that. Maria was left wearing a push up lace trimmed black bra, with her stockings and garter belt, black lace panties and a pair of black heels ... she walked slowly over to him.

"Wait" said Xander "sei così bella, you are so stunning please turn around for me, there is no rush we have all the night".

Xander wanted to make the most of every detail, he had a real desire to take pictures of her, she was that stunning, but he could not ask her that, this was their first night together. He was rock hard in his trousers and his mouth was actually salivating at the sight of her.

Maria knew she looked good and turned slowly around, turning her head to look at him over her shoulder, feeling the garter belt moving over her ass. She could see the admiration on his face and she could feel his whole being, taut with held back desire. She had never been able to sense a man like she could with Xander, it was an electric connection between them.

Slowly she turned around again and Xander just stared slowly from her heeled feet, up her long athletic legs, past the stockings, as his eyes followed the garter belt clips leading up to the pertest booty he had ever seen ... he was overwhelmed with sexual desire of course but also with disbelief at such a perfect body; on someone else the outfit would have looked slightly tarty but on her it just looked classy and desirable. She looked like a dancer, the way she held herself ...

"Maria you are the most beautiful woman I have ever seen" Xander murmured.

She turned and he admired her breasts in her black lace bra, he swallowed and felt almost like he was 18 again and she was his first girlfriend. He didn't want to disappoint this gorgeous woman. He beckoned her to come over to him.

Maria walked over to him and he got up from the sofa; he ran his lean masculine hands down her arms lightly and looked at her face. She reached for his shirt buttons and undid all of them. As his black shirt fell open it was Maria's turn to be breathless at just the first glimpse of his body. She had seen from the way he moved, fully clothed, that he obviously worked out, but his physique was incredible. He also had that slightly olive skin that promised a beautiful sexy tan if he was in the Italian sun for a couple of days. He moved his hands to her butt and caressed its curves slowly and sensually. They were intuitively wanting to take their time, although both had been consumed all evening with the building desire for each other.

As he touched her butt then moved back to her waist and around to her breasts she gasped as he discovered her body. Maria touched his muscular smooth chest and ran her hands down the centre of his torso, which had a light covering of dark hair, down to his trousers. She felt Xander breathe in fast as she undid his trousers.

He put his hands up to her face and cupped her face in his hands as he leant down to kiss her, lightly at first then more urgently. At the same time Maria opened the front of his trousers and touched his hardness for the first time, through his boxers. Xander continued kissing her, harder than before, as she ran her fingers along his length, pushing back his trousers until they fell to the floor so that she had a better grasp of his bulging erection. He felt very large to her touch, and extremely hard, she could feel him pulsating under her fingers.

Xander, still kissing her, found her bra clasp and undid it, releasing her breasts and pert nipples. Maria could hear her heart pounding and her breathing was uneven. Xander bent to take one of her nipples in his mouth and she gasped, as he sucked on her nipples she felt an answering shock of desire in her clit.

Xander stood back and took their glasses of champagne, giving her hers, staring at her. Once again without losing eye contact, he took a sip and bent to kiss her, again sharing the exquisite liquid with her as they kissed.

Xander took her hand and led her into the bedroom, he positioned himself behind her and pushed her lightly onto the bed. Maria moved forwards slowly across the bed on all fours, knowing exactly how sexy she looked from this direction wearing stockings, garter belt and heels as she moved onto the bed … Xander just watched her rounded ass swaying, taking in every single detail of this beautiful woman as she sexily moved over the high quality cotton sheets and positioned herself on the silk cushions, looking at him.

Xander stood at the end of the bed, still in his black shirt and boxers. The bedroom was lit only with the two bedside lamps. He knew he looked good but he really wanted to impress Maria, who was watching him intently from the bed. He bent to take off his boxers which were bulging and as he released his member he kept eye contact with her and he saw her mouth drop open slightly ... Xander knew he was fairly well endowed, but as his hardness was now free of the boxers and he felt the heaviness swing free, he saw from her face she was impressed.

Maria thought this week in Paris had already had its fair share of surprises, but she had never seen a guy this big, it was long and had an impressive girth, it was also extremely hard. She gazed at him with undisguised primeval desire as he stood at the end of the bed, her eyes moving from his face and its angular good looks and long black hair, to his well-defined shoulder muscles, hard chest and muscular torso, down to his athletically muscled legs with the biggest member she had ever seen arching keenly between them... bending one stockinged leg up sexily she reached for a sip of champagne to savour the moment as she took in the view of the sexy Italian man in front of her.

Xander moved with athletic grace onto the bed and placed his hands either side of her hips; with his shirt still on and his chest showing he looked like James Bond half undressed in a steamy sex scene. Slowly he bent his head and started to kiss her stomach, running his tongue down to her mound and kissing her through the lace as her hips moved sensually at his touch. Then, slowly, he pulled her panties down over her stockings and to her feet. As the panties were discarded on the floor he caressed her feet, still in stiletto heels and moved back up the bed towards her. He ripped off his shirt and threw it on the floor, reached for his champagne glass, took a small sip and bent his head to her pussy ... he let some drops of champagne fall from his sensual mouth onto her clit and as the cold liquid touched her, then ran down between her lips Maria moaned softly. He licked the champagne from her clit slowly, then faster as Maria gasped ... he took it into his mouth and sucked slowly, flicking his tongue at the same time. Slowly he moved down her shaved mound and slowly licked her lips which were already swollen and wet, with champagne and desire; again and again he darted his tongue just inside her.

Xander could taste how ready she was for him and he slowly inserted two fingers inside her, moving them from side to side slowly. Maria breathed in sharply as he then gently added a third finger and pushed them up inside her as far as he could reach, before making circular motions. She could feel herself stretching and lengthening, becoming ready for him. Maria reached for his hair and pulled him up towards her, then told him to lie down on the bed, she did not want to reach a climax too soon, although she could easily have done so already. She wanted to wait.

She admired his body as he lay on the bed, Xander had the same taut muscular athlete's body as the basketballer she had dated, he really was stunningly attractive. His maleness and the scent of him just engulfed her senses as she leant down to take his member in her mouth for the first time. He groaned as he felt her lips touch his cock, her tongue licked his head, then around the lip before moving sensually down his shaft. She ran her tongue back up again and had to stretch her mouth wide open to take him in completely, he was huge. She held his head in her mouth while her tongue slowly moved from side to side again and again on the underside where it joined the shaft. He groaned with pleasure. She tasted the unmistakeable salty taste of clear pre-cum which turned her on unbelievably, she was going to have to be careful with him as they were both so turned on.

As she took as much of him as possible into her mouth, teased him with her tongue, then ran her mouth down his shaft to take his full balls in her mouth, Xander didn't know how long he was going to be able to last with this woman. He had a strong primeval desire just to make her his own, quickly, forcefully and very deeply, but he also wanted to last all night.

She left his enormous member pulsating and kissed his stomach all the way up to his chest, where she took each of his nipples in her mouth, licking and teasing gently with her teeth. Xander's muscular chest rose up to meet her as he groaned "oh si si Maria".

She reached his mouth and he grabbed her face and kissed her with such ardent desire their lips crushed against each other. He pushed her up over him and in turn took each of her nipples in his mouth, sucking hard and licking so erotically she gasped out loud. He held her breasts with his hands as he sucked at her nipples, taking as much of her breast in his mouth as he could. Maria could feel the twitch in her clit as if there was a pleasure hotline direct from her breasts to between her legs. As they kissed again she lay on top of him, she could feel his hard erection pressing against her pussy. She felt so wet and open as if her whole body wanted to merge with his, right now.

Xander did not want to take her like that, so as she was kissing him, he reached over her body with his strong muscular arms and easily flipped her onto her back. He lay on top of her kissing and kissing her, then raised himself up to look at her.

Maria was lying on the bed, her dark hair wild on the pillow, her blue eyes dark with desire for him, he admired her pert breasts, flat stomach and gazed with desire at her long legs, still in garter belt, stockings and heels.

"I want you Maria" he breathed heavily "I want you now".

"I want you too Xander" she tried to control her breathing "take me"

Xander ran his hands down her legs and grasped her ankles, kissing each of her feet through the stockings, the sight of the black heels turning him on so much he felt on fire. He had to control himself, he couldn't remember the last time he wanted a woman this much.

He kept eye contact with her as he moved his huge member between her legs, while holding her legs open with his hands ... as his huge head touched her pussy and pushed slightly, Maria moaned "omigod yes Xander". He knew he was large and did not do as his primeval self was urging him, which was to take her immediately, and hard, instead he teased her by pushing only his head just inside her then pulling out. He pushed himself again just inside her, and back, then, as he felt her hips arching to meet him he pushed in further still ... Maria felt her pussy being entered and stretched and felt every inch of him as he pushed further into her body. She wanted him so badly but knew he was taking it slow at first as his member was so enormous. She felt herself open and lengthen and felt as if this sensual man was invading her belly so deeply. She felt every single inch of him as his thick member filled her completely. She felt him reach the very depths of her and just as she was wondering if she could take any more of him, she felt his full balls touch her perineum and she knew she had all of him. He pressed hard into her and started to make circular motions with his hips, Maria held his buttocks and they kissed hard as he moved slowly, deep deep within her, stretching her, making her fully ready for him. He was so deep inside her.

"Take me Xander take me" Maria gasped digging her nails into his buttocks as she was overcome with the desire to be taken by this man.

"I want you so bad Maria, I'm gonna take you now".

He started moving in and out of her, slowly at first but then faster. She felt him leave her open pussy, felt every inch of him moving out, then felt him stretch her again as he pushed back in. Faster and faster he moved. Maria was amazed at the depth of her own pussy, she felt totally consumed, as if her belly was entirely full of Xander's massive member as he pumped into her again and again.

She felt his breathing get more ragged and hers was the same.

"I am going to cum" she gasped as she felt him drawing near to his climax.

He took her harder and harder, pumping her full of his hardness again and again. Maria opened her legs as far as she could, wanting him to take her fully. Her long legs still in stilettoes were open either side of Xander's strong upper body. He was sweating slightly and his dark hair was swinging wildly around his face. She reached up and ran her hands over his sexy muscular shoulders while he plundered her hard and fast. She could feel how stretched she was every time he moved out of her and the feeling of being entirely filled by his enormous size turned her on like never before. She felt herself start to build and she could tell by the sound of his breathing he was the same. The level of desire that had been building all evening had breached its banks and there was no stopping it now. He put his head back, started to groan, then looked straight into her eyes.

She held his gaze while opening her legs still further, her pussy gripping him, feeling him rubbing against her G-spot as he drove deep into the depths of her. He took her harder and harder, finally letting his primeval desire overwhelm him, he couldn't help it, he needed to make her his. He took her as if he were a mediaeval warrior making this woman his own. She just wanted him to consume her totally and felt the wave of climax approaching. As she started to orgasm in waves and waves she cried out, still keeping eye contact as she saw him gasping with his mouth open, pumping her hard, his dark eyes wild with desire as he cried "si, si oh yes" and finally rammed so hard into her that she felt herself almost split apart by his size and felt him empty his tight balls up into her again and again. He seemed to cum for a long time, crying out, and finally dropped down onto her, still tightly inside her, and kissed her neck, then her cheek, then her mouth once more.

They lay like that for some time, not speaking, his hot sperm starting to drip out of her as he lost his hardness and her pussy let it release. She felt totally taken, completely owned by this man. She felt his member moving inside her, shrinking and finally slipping out of her, still heavy, followed by a fountain of hot love juice that ran out and down between her legs and onto the bed. He turned to the side of her and gently took her in his arms, kissed her again and again and folded her into his strong arms. He reached down and pulled the sheets up over them. They fell asleep in each other's arms, completely spent.

▲ ▲ ▲

CHAPTER SIX

▲

THE BOIS DE BOULOGNE

February 15

Xander woke first and for a second forgot where he was, before remembering with a naughty half smile the night before. He could hear the rain outside, falling strongly on the Parisian rooftops and against the window.

At the memory of their first night together he grew instantly hard, and in the half-light cast by the early morning sun tentatively peeping in through the curtains he reached over quietly and caressed Maria's shoulder and lightly kissed it; she had her back to him. He moved towards her slowly, running his hand lightly down to her waist and pulling her hips against his thighs and taut male hardness. Maria murmured slightly and pressed herself back against him. Xander reached down and put his heavy member between her legs while he kissed her shoulder again, kissing her neck. His pulsating erection slipped over the entrance to her pussy which was still wet from the previous night as they had gone straight to sleep in each other's arms. He reached around and found her breasts, cupping them in his hands and squeezing her nipples gently. Maria grasped his hand and pulled it to her, inserting one of his fingers into her mouth. As she moved her mouth in and out sensuously over his finger, Xander moved his hips and pushed his member gently into her wet pussy, as Maria breathed in sharply.

As he had done the night before, he played at her entrance while moving in and out of her gently, before he then pushed more firmly inside her, feeling her tight moistness gripping him as he entered her. He pulled out slightly and then went gently deeper and deeper, feeling himself fill her so fully he knew he had to be careful. Once again Maria felt every single inch of him and marvelled at the depth he was stretching her to, she had never taken a guy this big inside her. She felt as if she were being stretched apart as far as she could take and felt her clit twitch with desire. Xander gave a low moan as he pushed the last inch of his maleness between her legs, and felt his balls against her lips, and her clit which was already hard. She reached down and touched her clit, before cupping his balls in her hand and squeezing them. They were full and very heavy with the promise of more hot love juice. She felt him push into her again, up until now he had not fully pulled back out, he was totally inside her, waiting for her to lengthen and soften, her lips engorged with desire, before he would move in and out. Her fingers reached down and felt her open pussy, stretched to the limit as she touched his hardness that was forcing her lips apart. She moved two fingers apart to feel the width of him, he was so thick it felt as if he was splitting her open between her thighs. She groaned with pleasure as he started to pull out, the sensation was so intense she knew she could already cum whenever she wanted to but held herself back.

Outside the rain was falling harder, the storm was drenching Paris in a deluge of cleansing rain. Thunder started to boom in the threatening dark purple clouds over the city.

Xander pulled half out then pushed strongly back fully into her, and then again, as she pressed her hips back towards him. Half out, back in, then he pulled out fully and just entered her with his head, moving fast in and out. Maria gasped with pleasure as her lips were stretched and pushed in and out.

"Take me Xander, give it to me" she commanded him.

Xander did not need any encouragement, he played at her entrance once more then pushed his whole pulsating hard member deep right into her then straight back out and back in again. Maria screamed into her pillow with desire, she felt as if he were consuming her totally, that her belly was entirely full of him. He must have been reaching beyond her belly button inside of her and the thought he was so deep in her turned her on unbelievably. He started to pump really hard into her, rhythmic strokes, out to her lips and back into her belly, over and over again. On and on he pumped, his hardness wild and out of control, his need to take her was all consuming; their bodies were moving together, her hips crashing back into his as if to take even more of him into her body. Xander did not want to cum immediately and slowed down slightly.

"I want you so much Maria, I have to wait"

"Don't stop Xander don't stop"

Suddenly she felt his hand on her butt while he stayed inside her, not moving so fast, and a strong finger was playing between her ass cheeks, trying to find its target. As his finger found her ass she gasped again, he rubbed sensuously then licked his finger and inserted it just a little inside. Maria groaned. As he started pumping into her again with his huge member, slowly then faster, he pushed his finger into her ass at the same time and started moving it from side to side. Maria felt as if she had two members, both trying to consume her at the same time; the thought was so erotic.

"Omigod Xander you are going to make me cum so hard, fill me"

Xander loved that she talked to him, many women were not comfortable speaking aloud, but it really turned him on.

"And you are going to be filled my sexy Maria I am going to take you hard now are you ready?"

"Omigod yes" she gasped.

Xander kept his finger inside her ass and started to take her with an intensity that made Maria feel like her whole inside was just focused on absorbing this man, she cried out loud as he rammed his hardness deep into her again and again, pulling right out and pounding back in over and over. Her pussy felt as if it could not stretch widthwise or lengthwise anymore, yet then he started to feel even harder and thicker and she knew he was about to cum.

"Go on give it to me" she cried.

"You're gonna get it, it's coming" he breathed raggedly through his teeth.

The tempest outside was raging. The rain was beating against the windows and the thunder was crashing. Lightning was splitting the air outside, releasing the pressure of the storm directly over the centre of Paris.

Maria could feel herself building, the pressure inside her and the constant pounding in her pussy from his member were inflaming her right to the depths of her belly, and she felt him grow harder. She reached down to touch his balls again and they were so tight she knew he had to release soon. As his breathing became even more ragged, Maria reached down and touched her clit with her fingers, she knew they could cum together and the desire consumed her as she pressed her clit from side to side.

"Oh Maria si si siii" he groaned as he realised she was playing with herself.

He pumped and pumped into her, holding her hips and pulling her against him with every heaving motion into her body, Maria could feel her mound and pussy pulsating in waves out over her belly as she started to cum and she cried out. He took her again and again and cried out loud as his huge member thrust once more so deeply into her as he discharged all his juice so hard she could feel it shooting into her, deep in her belly. As he came and came she pressed her clit over again and writhed against him, cumming against his member deep in her, gripping him from the inside as she twitched all over, lost in the throes of a long orgasm.

Neither of them spoke as he grew smaller inside her then pulled out as his juice ran from her like a flood, over her leg and onto the sheets. Xander reached for her, turning her to him for the first time that morning to look at her, kissed her on the lips then on the cheek then folded her in his arms, holding her tight not saying a word.

He was shocked at the intensity of their lovemaking, after only last night and this morning. It didn't feel as if they had only just met, it was the sort of chemistry you get when you know someone really well. He had an insatiable urge to keep on taking her, to make her his own, over and over again. He had not felt like this for a very long time and if he was being honest, although it was incredible, he did not want to risk falling for anyone seriously, particularly someone who lived 7000km away. This American girl was having a very strong effect on him. For now he held her close and felt her arm around his chest reach up and caress his face. He kissed her fingers and they fell into a sort of half-sleep.

**

When they woke the rain had stopped and the light was coming more strongly through the curtains, although it was still early.

"Let's shower together" Maria suggested with a naughty look on her face.

She took his hand and led him into her huge marble shower, where they soaped each other, she sensuously moving her hands over his muscled back and shoulders, down over his smooth muscular ass and caressing his manhood, which even when "soft" was not at all small.

"You are a very impressive size Xander, so sexy, you have an incredible body" she murmured.

"And you have a dream body Maria, you are just perfect" he replied, running his hands from her waist over her pert booty, he really could not believe she was 48. If you had blindfolded him and made him guess, just from touching her he would have guessed about 38, maybe less.

Even after such a sexy start to the morning, Xander could feel himself re-hardening at the touch of her hands under the flow of water. Maria was still turned on, even though her pussy was feeling swollen and pummelled from his onslaught the night before and this morning.

Xander felt between her legs with his fingers, finding her lips still engorged and inserted two digits gently inside her. He played with her pussy then turned her around so her back was to him, and as he kissed her neck he inserted his thumb gently into her ass, moving his fingers inside her pussy. Maria gasped as he pushed his thumb up into her. Xander once again had a mental image of taking her in this tight forbidden place, and groaned at the thought.

Maria turned back to him and bent her knees, moving into a crouching position, and took his half hard member in her mouth, licking its length and moving rhythmically down its shaft with her hand. As she did so she looked up at him with her eyes full of desire. Xander looked down at her, her beautiful mouth stretched open to take as much of his cock in as possible, he thrust gently and felt his shaft touch the back of her throat. Maria continued to lick him, pulling him out of her mouth to spit on the end of his cock then lick it off … Xander was so turned on, he felt harder than he could remember, so close to this sexy woman he only met two days ago. He reached down and took his member out of her mouth and started to brush it over her mouth, tapping her cheeks with its heavy weight, before putting it back into her mouth. Maria had her hands gripping his ass while he used his hand to push his member in and out of her mouth, faster and faster.

"I want to cum on your face" he gasped.

"Yes yes do it Xander" Maria looked up at him.

He pumped his hand faster and faster, Maria opening her mouth ready for him, licking him constantly with her tongue as his head entered her mouth again and again … Xander felt himself building again and started to groan "si si" as he felt his orgasm coming … Maria pulled back from him just as he started to shoot his juice all over her face, catching some in her mouth and letting him spurt all over her. She felt the hot juice running down her face and reached with her tongue to taste it and swallow it, tasting the saltiness.

Xander reached down and pulled her to standing, desire fierce in his eyes. Turning her, still half hard he inserted himself into her pussy from behind, holding himself in her with his hips while he played with her nub with his fingers, the other hand coming around to insert two fingers into her pussy, with his softening member. His member was so long, even only half hard he could fill her without slipping out. He could feel the cum still on his cock as he pushed his fingers into her from the front and found her g-spot. Maria could feel him pushing into her from behind, her pussy still feeling used, she could feel his semi hard member. His strong fingers were exploring inside her at the same time and as he opened her lips, firmly massaging her g-spot her pussy just melted into orgasm after orgasm. She could still taste his saltiness in her mouth, could feel his sperm on her face, as she came in waves of desire, taken by his fingers and his heavy member at the same time.

He turned her back to face him and they finished the shower with a long sensual kiss, under the hot water, before getting out and putting on the soft white robes.

**

Xander got dressed and prepared to leave her suite, then turned to her.

"Maria I know it is early, but I am going to take Zeus to the Bois de Boulogne for a walk this morning, would you like to come with me?"

"OK that would be lovely" Maria replied, she had not planned to visit the large park on the west of Paris but she had heard it was very beautiful, about twice the size of Central Park.

"If you like, we could get breakfast there, maybe some pastries and coffee in one of the cafés in the park?" Xander suggested.

**

They met in the lobby half an hour later and made their way outside to where his Maserati had been brought over from the garage across the road.

Maria got into the passenger side while Xander loaded Zeus into the back. The car was fairly new and she could smell a mixture of his Dior Sauvage perfume and the leather interior, the scent was intoxicating. Xander slipped athletically into the driver's side and as he turned on the engine the stereo immediately burst into life with Andrea Bocelli's 'Canto della Terra', which Maria absolutely loved. Xander's muscled legs in his jeans, coupled with his lean tanned hands on the driving wheel made her belly pulsate again with desire, this guy was so sexy.

"Guarda questa ter-rrr-aaa che, che gira anche per noi » Xander was singing again as he drove off.

"My love che sei l'amore mio, sento la tua voce e ascolto il mare" he stopped suddenly and looked at her "do you know this song?"

"Of course" said Maria.

"Do you understand all the words Maria?" he asked, glancing at her with a dark brooding look in his eyes.

"No not really, not all of them" she admitted.

"You should know the meaning" he said, then changed the subject as he navigated the traffic.

Maria felt such a happiness in her soul as she drove with the most gorgeous Italian man she had ever seen, in his Maserati, through the stunning streets of Paris, listening as Andrea Bocelli's voice became more and more dramatic as the song went on. Xander glanced over at her, his teeth white against his tanned face as he grinned at her, she was sure she could read his mind as she naughtily smiled back at him, remembering the start to the morning.

They drove through to the Trocadero roundabout then around to the exit for Avenue Georges Mandel which led in a straight line out to the Bois de Boulogne as they headed west through the 16th Arrondissement. Zeus was panting loudly anticipating his morning walk but was safely contained behind a dog guard, on his travel bed. They arrived and Xander parked, there were very few people there as it was partly cloudy and now raining lightly again, as they set off through the woods with Zeus.

Maria knew that the Fondation Louis Vuitton, an art gallery with a beautiful shallow cascading pool at its entrance, was to the right, but they took a path leading west through the trees. Xander reached for her hand and they walked for a while not speaking, just appreciating the calming energy of the trees and the damp earthy smell of the plants after the rain. Zeus had run ahead, sniffing, as they approached one of the lakes. They stopped by the water's edge and Xander turned Maria to him, put his strong arms around her and looked at her. She looked into his dark brown eyes, once again full of desire for her. Maria had minimal make-up on, just a golden primer, smooth base and light eye makeup, but a brief ray of light coming through the trees gave her eyes an even brighter shade of turquoise.

"Maria you have such beautiful eyes they are so pretty, like gemstones" Xander was just staring at her, he didn't want to remember that after tomorrow he more than likely would never see her again.

He bent his head to kiss her lips, pulling her tightly to him so she could feel his hard body pressed against hers. He was so tall and strong. They kissed slowly, then as their tongues writhed strongly together Xander kissed her hard, moving his hand behind her head to press her to him, then putting his hands on her cheeks to hold her while he kissed her. They stayed like that for several minutes, oblivious to the occasional jogger on the path behind them. Maria could feel his hardness thrusting in his jeans and felt herself melt inside with desire. This guy could turn her on instantly, it was unbelievable the effect he had on her.

The kiss slowed and Xander bent his head still further to kiss her neck softly as they pulled apart and made their way back to the path and a small café where they ordered coffee and croissants.

The Bois de Boulogne was, in times past, a hunting ground for deer and wild boar (sanglier as the French called them) for the kings of France. The forest still had quite a wild feel about it, although the carefully maintained lake and manicured paths had brought it into modern day Parisian life. It is known as the "lungs of Paris" as the city has a worsening pollution problem. Many Parisians used the park, especially in summer, although it was apparently to be avoided late at night. You could see why, Maria thought, there were plenty of dark hidden areas in the thick trees.

As they walked back towards the car park, Maria decided to ask Xander something.

She had planned to visit a museum later, a small one, and she had suddenly felt as if she would like to share the experience with Xander. As they circled back through the trees around the lake hand in hand to the car, she asked him.

"Xander would you like to visit the Jacquemart-André museum with me later today?"

"What is the Jacquemart-André?" Xander asked.

Maria explained that the Musée Jacquemart-André on Boulevard Haussmann was a previously private collection of artwork that had been opened to the public in 1913 after the death of portrait painter Cornélie "Nélie" Jacquemart. Maria thought the story of how the collection had come to be was quite romantic. In 1872 the young Nélie had been commissioned to paint the portrait of Edouard André, who was from a wealthy family of bankers and was involved in politics with Napoléon III.   Nélie was not from an aristocratic background. There is apparently no proof that they had a relationship, but she married him nine years after painting his portrait. Maria liked to think that she had had a secret affair with the dashing Edouard, probably against his family's wishes, before marrying. They did not have children and in the 13 years they spent travelling together through Europe, Turkey and Egypt, they collected over 200 sculptures and around 100 paintings. They had an agreement that after they had both died, the collection would be left to the Institut de France, which manages various things, including many museums and chateaux which are now open to the public. You can visit their beautiful home and admire the huge personal collection of art, as well as the stunning architecture and design of the classical townhouse itself.

"Actually Xander they apparently have a whole room dedicated to the artwork of the Florentines and Venetians as the couple were huge admirers of Italian art" Maria smiled.

"That would be great" he smiled at her, "I have another business lunch today, so would it be OK for you if we went late afternoon?"

As Xander's meeting was in the same area, they decided they would meet for a coffee at the rooftop café of the Printemps department store at the bottom of Boulevard Haussmann around 4pm and then go to the museum from there. Maria planned to go back to the hotel, change, have a room service snack lunch then head over to Printemps and the other shops in that area to do some shopping, before meeting Xander.

They got back to the Maserati and Zeus jumped in the back. Xander held the door open for Maria and as she moved to get in, he took her in his arms and slowly kissed her. They stayed like that, oblivious to time and space as their tongues urgently explored each other. Eventually they pulled apart and looked at each other, both thinking of the previous night and this morning. He kissed her gently on the mouth again, then got into the car.

"This time the music is for you Maria" said Xander, as he put Bruce Springsteen's "The Rising" on the stereo.

"I adore Springsteen how did you know!?" she exclaimed, it was as if Xander just instinctively knew her, the times they were spending together were almost like déjà vu.

They headed back to the hotel, Xander expertly driving the Maserati through the Parisian traffic.

"Maria I would really like to see you tonight as well, if you want?" he paused slightly, "I have my meeting now and then I need to make some calls early evening, after we have been to the museum, but maybe we could meet later, after?" he looked at her again "I do not want to take up all your time on your holiday Maria, of course, but I am driving back to Italy tomorrow night after my final meeting, tonight is my last night here."

"Yes, I would like that very much" she looked at him and he smiled at her, his dark brown eyes looking sensuously at her. She just melted inside looking at him and although she kept inwardly kicking herself at her inability to stick with her own plans to avoid guys for a while, she could not wait to spend more time with him. What a shame she would not see him again after tonight, he really was so gorgeous.

She smiled to herself as the Bose stereo system belted out "come on up for the rising, come on up for the rising tonight", she wasn't sure if Xander realised what she was smiling about as he glanced sexily at her then concentrated on driving through the heavy traffic.

Once back at the hotel, she ordered a sandwich lunch and relaxed for a while in her suite. She sent some photos and messages, but NYC would still be asleep at this hour of their morning. Anyway, she thought, if she got hold of any of her friends now they would want to know all the details. She giggled out loud to herself as she imagined Lisette's reaction to the latest update on Maria's "holiday romance".

▲ ▲ ▲

CHAPTER SEVEN

▲

THE SECRET

February 15, later that afternoon

Maria left the hotel, crossed over the Champs-Elysées and found the Franklin D. Roosevelt metro stop. Once on the train she stayed on for a couple of stops on Line 9, getting off at Saint Augustin. From there she wandered down towards Printemps. She knew Printemps was a bit like Macy's and she remembered photos from Christmastime she had seen during her research about Paris of their huge Christmas tree that stretched all the way up through the central atrium to the stunning stained glass dome at the top. She did some shopping, trying things on here and there, then made her way up to the top floor where the café was located. Outside on the terrace there was an incredible view of Paris. She could see the Sacré-Coeur behind her, on the Montmartre hilltop, while to the south west over the endless roofs she could see the Eiffel Tower, among other beautiful church spires and domes. She ordered a coffee and sat at one of the tables on the edge, admiring the view.

Xander finished his meeting in rue des Mathurins, where he successfully signed several contracts with the new client. Xander was a fairly ruthless businessman, not afraid to speak his mind. He was very happy with the way business had gone these last few days, the client was eager to start construction. Although Xander spoke some French, one of the managers had spoken fluent Italian, so they had gelled well together. It makes it so much easier when you connect. Every deal was different, but he had been very successful over the last twenty years and the business had given him a good standard of living. He made his way through the streets to Printemps and went directly up to the top floor, looking for Maria as he entered the café. He saw her outside before she saw him, she was taking pictures of the beautiful Sacré-Coeur which looked particularly picturesque from this viewpoint. He admired how she was standing, leaning on one leg so that her butt was set off to perfection in her jeans. She really was stunning and he felt the butterflies in his stomach again as he looked at her. He really must pull himself together though, he thought, he felt so close to her but really "this", whatever it was they had going on together, was unlikely to continue.

Maria turned round as Xander came to meet her, holding her upper arms gently as he kissed her cheek. They had coffee, then made their way back inside the store and down to the street. They jumped on a bus to take them part of the way up the very long Boulevard Haussmann. Maria remembered reading that Eugène Georges Haussmann, or Baron Haussmann, designed and started construction of the boulevard in 1857. Napoléon III wanted to create a "new" Paris with long straight wide boulevards, and many of the more ancient smaller buildings and roads were demolished to make way for the Paris we know today.

They got off halfway up as the Musée Jacquemart-André was located at 158 Boulevard Haussmann. Maria looked up at 19th century townhouse which was slightly elevated above the street; it was truly beautiful. They went in through the door in the high wall and paid, then made their way to the back of the house where the entrance was located; the back was just as stunning as the front. Xander reached for her hand and leant down to kiss her neck as they made their way into the first room. There was a self-portrait of Nélie displayed at the start, and Maria thought she looked very brooding, like she was guarding a precious secret.

It was February and the museum was not full so as they moved along the mezzanine balcony over the ballroom and over to the ornate staircase, Xander pulled her to him, kissing her passionately on the lips. In this setting, with the old polished wooden floorboards, the beautiful paintings and the classic architecture of the house, Maria could easily imagine another time, another century in Paris, where the young portrait painter fell in love with her subject ... eventually marrying him years later.

As they made their way back past the sculptures and headed for the exit, a family was in front of them with a couple of small children and a baby in a pushchair. Maria joked how glad she was not to have small kids anymore, seeing the parents constantly keeping an eye on their kids.

"Imagine Xander, some people our age do have kids under ten, if they started a family late" she said "I adored my girls at that age but I can't imagine having small kids now" Maria laughed.

"It depends on circumstances I suppose" Xander said, darkly, his handsome face suddenly clouding over.

"I bet Gianni and Marco were double trouble when they were younger weren't they?" she asked him.

He seemed agitated as he answered abruptly "oh yes, they kept me busy" but added nothing more and walked ahead of her out of the museum.

Maria was surprised. Of course, they had only met each other three days ago, they were strangers really, but he had never seemed this offhand with her before. She followed him out onto the street where he turned to her, staring at her with such a dark look on his face she was worried.

"Maria, I want to talk to you" he said.

"OK Xander, of course, what do you want to talk about?" Maria replied.

"Let's find a bar, we can talk over a drink, I need one" he murmured.

Maria wondered what on earth had made his mood change so quickly and then remembered it was right after she had commented about the family with young kids. Thinking about it he had also seemed slightly distant when she had mentioned small kids the other day, but she could not imagine why that would be. She reached for his hand and they walked into the labyrinth of backstreets that lie between the Champs-Elysées and Boulevard Haussmann, where they found a secluded, low-lit bar. It was half empty and there were plenty of tables free. Xander led the way to a private table towards the back. The waiter approached and Xander asked Maria if she minded if he ordered.

"Go ahead Xander" she was confused now and even more so when Xander ordered two shots of golden tequila, she hadn't taken him for a tequila guy! He was looking really worried though, and Maria reached for his hand across the table.

"Xander what on earth is wrong, tell me" she said.

He reached for the shot of tequila and downed it in one. Maria sipped hers, golden tequila was actually delicious.

"Maria I have something to tell you, I know after today we probably will not see each other again, and especially after I tell you this, but I want you to know something".

Maria stared at him, confused, although she had sensed there was something he was agitated about.

"Only two people know about this at the moment, my brothers, but I feel I can trust you and I want to tell you. I don't know why, because we only just met, but I want to tell you, is that OK?" he said, darkly.

Maria was intrigued and slightly worried "of course Xander you can tell me anything you like" she told him.

"I don't know how to start" Xander said "so I will just tell you".

"OK" Maria said.

"Nine years ago, it was not good between me and my wife. I am not proud of this, but I had an affair with a woman I met through work, she was from Verona. We saw each other for about six months, we didn't use protection because she didn't have kids and told me she could not have any. She had no brothers or sisters and she had fairly old parents. She said she thought her family were genetically infertile. Anyway, after six months we stopped seeing each other and that was it. My wife never knew I had cheated, it was the end of it. My boys were only 11 when I was seeing her".

Maria could already see where this was going, she wanted to hold his hand but she just let him talk.

"So this was a long time ago, OK, I had forgotten all about her, I left my wife six years after the affair, when Gianni and Marco were 17. I stayed with her that long because of them really, they both went a bit crazy when they were 15 and I didn't want to put them through a break up as well as everything else".

"Yes I understand, lots of people stay for the kids" Maria said.

"Then, just after Christmas, six weeks ago, the woman contacted me" Xander stopped talking and put his elbows on the table and his hands to his face, looking at Maria over his fingers, the pain showing clearly in his face.

"You know what I am going to say, my Maria, don't you" he said, reaching for her tequila, downing it too, and signalling the bartender for another two drinks.

"She had a baby didn't she" Maria said quietly.

She felt very emotional just looking at him, his eyes looked so hurt.

"Maria, she had twins!" Xander's eyes were glistening and he looked away as the bartender brought their drinks over.

"Oh my goodness" Maria said, staring at him.

"So they are twin girls, their names are Celestina and Alessandra, and they were 8 years old last October" he said "she wanted me to meet them, she sounded strange, like she was really down, not at all how I remembered her" he looked pensive "she told me how sorry she was, how she had thought it best not to say anything, because I had a wife and kids, so she kept it secret and brought them up on her own. She didn't ask me for money, just wanted me to meet them, and she wants me to be part of their lives now, she says she made a mistake keeping their papa from them", he looked at Maria, the pain showing in his eyes.

"So have you met them?" Maria asked.

"Yes, three weeks ago" said Xander "so I told Antonio and Cristo what happened and I am going to Rome next week to tell Chiara in person. I don't want to tell her over the phone" Xander was babbling now "then I need to tell Gianni and Marco they have two sisters … their mother is going to freak out … I went to Verona to meet them" his voice was shaking.

This time Maria reached over and took both his hands "it's OK Xander, go on" she said.

"They are so beautiful Maria" he smiled "Katia, that's their mother, had told them their papa was coming to see them, I don't know what story she told them about me before, I don't know what reason she gave them for their papa never seeing them. I spent two hours with them, we went to the park, it was so strange. They were quite shy. Katia is typical northern Italian and blonde, but the twins are dark, just like me" he smiled at Maria "they look a bit like Gianni and Marco did when they were small" his eyes were sad.

"Xander that is some story" Maria said, sipping her tequila "I am so sorry, and I am sorry for all those things I said earlier about not having small children anymore, I had no idea, obviously".

"Oh, Maria please do not worry, you didn't know. Hell, I didn't know until six weeks ago!" he tried to joke, finishing his drink.

"Xander I wish there was something I could say" Maria said, gazing at him.

"So anyway, if you want to cancel our drinks tonight just tell me Maria, I will understand of course" Xander said, looking sideways at her with a crestfallen look on his face.

What was it about this gorgeous Italian, Maria didn't think there was anything that he could say that would put her off wanting to see him. This really was not how she had planned her week in Paris but right now she thought she may as well go with the totally different flow this trip had taken, for now anyway.

"Xander of course I would still like to meet you tonight" she said.

Xander smiled at her, grasping her hand.

"Maybe we could just get drinks and a platter of cheese and ham in that jazz bar around the corner from the hotel" she suggested, "instead of dinner".

Maria had noticed several people in the bars she had been past, eating delicious looking cheese and ham selections from slate platters, it seemed to be a bit like a sort of French tapas thing to do.

"That would be great" Xander said, hoping the relief was not showing on his face "we can meet in the bar later."

"Perfect" she said.

They got up and left the bar, and as Xander put his arm around her shoulders she slipped her arm under his jacket and around his waist. They walked like that right through to the top of the Champs-Elysées through the pretty side streets, it felt so natural, so perfect being with him. Maria just let herself enjoy the moment, as they made their way back to the hotel.

Xander went to take care of Zeus and make some calls. Maria went back to her suite, threw herself flat on her back on her bed and digested this latest development. She felt so sorry for Xander, and so helpless. She felt there should have been something she could do for him but they didn't even know each other very well, he was leaving in 24 hours' time to sort out this situation and she was flying back to NYC soon. She found it very touching he had wanted to tell her. He hadn't needed to. Maybe he felt the same connection she did. What a crazy week this had turned into.

**

Maria took the chance to go down to the hotel gym for a quick 5km on the treadmill. Normally while she was running her head cleared, but as she ran she did not feel calm, as she usually did, she sensed something. She didn't know what. She was quite intuitive and she sensed change, as if they were somehow not finished with all this. Poor Xander, what a shock that must have been. She hoped he and his boys would be OK, after he broke the news.

She tried to forget about Xander for a minute and thought about her final three days in Paris before her flight home. She planned to go right to the top of the Eiffel Tower tomorrow night, at dusk, as she had read you can see all the famous monuments start to be illuminated as night falls. Then she also wanted to visit the famous, if spooky, catacombs, which were full of exhumed bones of Parisians long past, after the cemeteries were dismantled to make way for new build as the city expanded. The area in Paris above the tunnels of bones had a strict weight limit on the size and height of buildings built over them, due to the hollow catacombs below. How creepy if you lived above them, she thought.

She was going to be busy the next few days and kicked herself yet again as she suddenly felt sad that Xander would have left and she would once again be exploring on her own … *"honestly Maria"* she said to herself *"OMG that was the whole POINT of coming here in the first place!!"*. She determined to once again become focused on her future in the time that she had left here in Paris. She had to treasure every memory, although now she was here, she knew she would bring Luisa and Carla back for a visit fairly soon, maybe for a Christmas visit. She had seen pictures of Paris, decorated with Christmas displays, the Champs-Elysées illuminated with lights. Yes, maybe she would do that at the end of this year. She finished her run with a sprint and quickly made her way back to her room to shower, before getting ready to meet Xander in the bar for their very last evening.

**

They met in the hotel bar but went straight out to find the jazz bar, which was not difficult as even before they turned a corner they could hear the melody of a superb sax solo drifting out onto the street as people opened the door to enter. They went in and found a place in the corner as the bar was already fairly full. It was low-lit and cosy, with black and white photos of famous jazz musicians adorning the walls. Maria did not actually know much about jazz, but she loved it, she felt immediately chilled out hearing the music. Xander ordered a bottle of Chardonnay and a platter of cheeses and hams to share, which arrived promptly accompanied by a delicious bowl of sliced French baguette. The band was really good, with a singer, a pianist, a bass player and the saxophone player.

Maria and Xander chatted about all sorts of things, not mentioning the situation with the girls. They held hands under the table and as Maria glanced at Xander as they were listening to the music, she sensed he was as absorbed in the moment as she was. He turned to her as he felt her looking at him and smiled, reaching up with one hand to turn her face to his.

"I am really enjoying this evening" he said looking intensely into her eyes, he seemed more relaxed since their conversation earlier.

"Me too" she replied as he pulled her face to his and started to kiss her gently.

The kiss went on for some time, very slow, very sensual and loving, and once again both of them felt as if time was standing still when they were together.

A bit later the band started to play some upbeat songs and people started to dance. Xander grabbed Maria's hand and laughing they went onto the very small dance floor by the tables and started to dance. The bar was so full they did not have much choice except to dance very closely together, with Xander placing one of his legs between hers as they moved with the rhythm. Once again, the electric attraction between them was palpable, she felt him hardening as he pulled her close to him as they danced.

"Shall we go back to the hotel?" Xander whispered in her ear then looked at her with a smouldering look in his eyes.

"Will you walk me to my suite?" she whispered back sexily as she licked his ear lightly.

"I will, just as soon as we go for one last walk with my dog" he joked.

Xander kissed her then they retrieved their things, paid, and made their way back to the hotel to take out Zeus.

It was gone midnight as they got in the elevator, Xander once again pinning her to the side of it and kissing her passionately. They were both hungry for each other, the desire so strong between them. There was also an urgency that had not been there before, as they were both well aware they were on a countdown of the time left together, before Xander left Paris. Maria felt herself becoming wet just at the thought of him and as she put her hands under his shirt and pulled his hips towards her, she could feel him so hard for her already.

He dropped Zeus in his suite and a couple of minutes later he came back and knocked on her door. Xander put his cell phone on the coffee table as Maria started to unbutton his shirt, both of them were already breathless with desire. He pulled her to him, his hands grasping her breasts through her dress then pulling it up over her hold-up stockings, his fingers lean and hard, finding her panties and pulling them to one side. Maria gasped as he thrust two digits into her, then a third, feeling her already so wet for him. With his fingers pushing deep in her pussy and his tongue pushing hard into her mouth, Maria felt herself already not far from an orgasm, this man was unbelievable.

Xander's cell on the table began to call and vibrate, which he ignored as he undressed Maria, gasping as he took in her dark purple lacy underwear she was wearing under her dress. He stood back to admire the sight of her, still in her heels.

"Maria you are so beautiful, I want you so bad" he breathed.

His cell started to ring again, stopped, but immediately re-started ringing and buzzing.

"I am so sorry Maria I am just going to see who is calling" he pulled away breathlessly.

As Xander answered his cell and the person on the other end started speaking loudly in rapid Italian, Xander sounded confused and Maria heard him say "polizia?" but then saw his face quickly turn white. She caught the words "incidente" and "gemelli" which she knew meant "accident" and "twins". As Xander glanced at her she could see the shock in his face as he was asking about his boys. But then he seemed to be questioning why they were talking about "dipartimento pediatrico dell'ospedale". Maria gathered his boys obviously would not have been in the children's department of the hospital, and she caught her breath, realising something must have happened to the twins he had just told her about. The girls nobody knew existed until six weeks ago and who he had only met once, just recently … but why were they calling him and not their mother. Maria felt a dark wave of apprehension come over her, the same feeling she had had while she was running earlier.

He hung up, looking at her in total shock, Maria could see he was trembling.

"Maria it's not Gianni and Marco. It's the girls, my twin girls. Maria, there has been a car accident, their mother has been killed outright, the girls are in intensive care. The police found my number in the girls' identification papers. He was shaking "I need to call my brothers".

"Oh Xander of course" Maria touched his arm and left him to call them.

Xander got through to Antonio and she could hear Antonio getting very agitated on the other end of the line. Then he called Cristofano and a similar exchange in loud rapid Italian went on for several minutes, Xander pacing and pacing, gesturing with his free hand and running it constantly through his wild black hair. Eventually they hung up and Maria came back from the bedroom, now wearing a bathrobe. Xander turned to her, his face white, then sat down on the sofa, his hands covering the lower part of his face as he looked up at her, totally shocked.

"Maria, they say I am their only living relative, the girls should be OK but after, they will be living with me. I need to get back to Italy tomorrow, Antonio is checking flights for me".

Xander looked up at her, his face tight with stress.

"Maria please, I need you to do one thing for me" he said, "can you ask Charles if I can pay him to drive my Maserati back to Firenze for me, with Zeus?"

"I am so sorry Xander" Maria said as she went to sit beside him, taking his hand "I will call him right now, he can take you to the airport first".

Xander called Antonio again while Maria went into the bedroom to call Charles.

Charles immediately agreed to come and pick up Signor Sabatini and take him to CDG airport tomorrow. Maria would look after Zeus until Charles came back from the airport, but Charles also shared some other information with Maria, which Maria would not tell Xander. No need to complicate matters right now she thought, Xander had enough to deal with, she would sort this out. She quietly made a quick call to Lisette. She had had the craziest idea. She explained her spur of the moment crazy plan.

"Whaaaat T F" came the scream from NYC "yes definitely OMG the poor guy".

They discussed things quickly and Lisette finished loudly with "GIRL POWER Maria, we can fix this, don't worry I got you".

"Can you sort everything out your end?" Maria asked, "then let me know times ASAP OK".

Maria hung up and let Lisette handle the rest.

She went back into the suite and told Xander Charles had agreed.

"Thank you Maria" Xander's face was shell shocked, he was trying to be rational and make logical decisions but he felt as if he had taken several full body blows. Were the girls badly hurt? What was he going to tell his family? Only his brothers knew about the girls at the moment. Antonio was going to call Chiara and tell her the news, this could not wait until Xander went to Rome. Tomorrow back in Italy he had no choice not only to tell his boys, immediately, but also with the news that their two newly announced little sisters would be coming to LIVE with them in less than a week! Xander was trying to process the ripple effect of this news and the people it was going to affect. He imagined his ex's reaction, she was going to go crazy. And at the back of his mind, even though they had only known each other a few days, he already knew Maria would not have been keen to date somebody with small kids, but a single father with sole responsibility for twin 8 year olds? Although he had not really thought any further ahead than perhaps inviting her to Italy and spending more time with her, he was suddenly very sad at the thought that she, of course, would not want to see him again. She would make some sensible but nice excuse about living in NYC 7000km away and it not being very realistic.

"Xander" Maria said, and he looked up at her with tears in his beautiful dark eyes.

Maria just went to him and took him in her arms.

"Things will work out eventually Xander, the girls will be OK, they will recover, and then after this bombshell has had time to settle, I am sure your family will understand. You are not the first man in the world to have unplanned children. You have to be incredibly strong; you are going to have two devastated little girls and two shocked boys. At least you will get to bring the girls up now, know them, making up for lost time. I don't know what else to say Xander I really don't", her voice broke.

They just held each other for a long time.

"I will go back to my suite" Xander said eventually "you need to rest and I don't want this explosion of my life to spoil the rest of your time in Paris".

"Xander do you really think I am going to sleep after all this?" Maria said, smiling gently at him "stay here with me, it's late already, we can just get some rest for a couple of hours then you can sort your bags in the morning".

"OK if you are sure" Xander did not want to be alone, if he was honest with himself. The shock of the news six weeks ago that he had not two children but four, when the mother of the girls had contacted him was bad enough, but this was obviously way worse. He remembered how he had felt when she had contacted him with the news, how he had broken out in a sweat and could not stop trembling. It was the same now. He also knew that he was counting down his last hours with Maria, this American woman he had known for precisely three days but who he felt so close to. The chemistry between them was like nothing else he had ever experienced. The sex was incredible of course, the desire for her just overwhelmed him, but he just wanted to be close to her, to talk to her, walk in silence with her, to do everything with her, she attracted him like no other woman ever had ... but they had only hours left together, then soon they would be on separate continents.

"I am going to shower then get into bed" Maria said "we can rest".

"OK" Xander replied quietly just as his cell rang and Antonio gave him the news that the earliest flight out of Paris he could get a seat was 13.00 the following day. The twins were in the paediatric department of Ospedale di Careggi in Firenze and Xander could go straight there from the airport.

They both showered quickly then, in contrast to the previous times they had both been in her bed, they just lay in each other's arms, not speaking. The room was lit by only one lamp and was very dark. Maria was digesting both his revelation this afternoon and the tragic news they had just received. She felt so sorry for him, she could not imagine what reaction his boys would have when he told them tomorrow. Xander was such a strong man, physically muscular and powerful, but she was seeing him at his most vulnerable right now. And selfishly, although he would have left tomorrow anyway, she felt a deep sadness that they only had hours left together before he left urgently for the airport.

They were facing each other, their heads nearly touching on the pillow and she stroked him gently, down the side of his muscular torso and over his hips, down his hard, lightly tanned leg ... and back up again ... she kissed him gently on the forehead ... despite himself Xander felt himself stir at her touch and moved his hips towards her. As Maria ran her hand back down to his hips her hand moved down to between his legs. His member was already engorged, lying heavily on the cotton sheet as she faced him.

"Maria what do you do to me" he murmured.

"Keep still" she told him.

She moved down the bed until her head was level with his throbbing member and, stretching her lips wide, took him in her mouth ... she was so turned on, despite the situation, and feeling his huge head in her mouth as she slowly moved her tongue around it she felt her clit twitch and her pussy moisten in anticipation. She sucked gently for a while, taking as much of him in her mouth as she could, feeling her jaw and cheeks stretch. Xander groaned as he became fully hard and reached down, pulling Maria back up towards him so he could kiss her. They kissed slowly for a long time, Xander pressing his body against hers but making no move to enter her. For a long time he just held her, kissing her mouth, her cheeks, her eyes, holding her hair as he kissed her deeply on the mouth. He pushed her further upwards so he could take her nipples into his mouth, sucking and sucking on them, holding her breasts as Maria held herself against the headboard. This man turned her to jelly, she felt the desire between them so keenly it was like a series of electric shocks. He pulled her back to kiss her mouth again and only then did he reach down with one hand and with a finger start to caress her nub.

Maria arched towards him as his fingers travelled down still further, seeking her moist entrance. He slipped two fingers inside her pussy and pushed them up inside her, slowly moving them in and out, before adding a third then a fourth finger as she gasped. He gently pushed his fingers up her, twisting in circles and opening and closing his fingers; Maria was sopping wet for him already but he wanted to make sure she was ready before he entered her with his huge size. She knew he was preparing her, making her ready for him and just at the thought of him inside her again she felt herself opening and lengthening.

"Oh Xander" Maria whispered.

He pulled his fingers gently from her, and brought them up to his mouth, keeping eye contact with her as he sucked her juice from his fingers then offered them to her to suck. She licked her own desire off his fingers as he moved over her, pushing her onto her back. He opened her legs and pushed them back so her knees bent slightly, and she saw him watching as her pussy opened for him as he pushed her thighs apart. Xander was taking his time, he didn't want to forget any of this, in the future he wanted to keep every detail of Maria safe in his memories as if it were yesterday. He placed his heavy member at her sopping entrance and moved his hips forward to enter her slowly. Maria gasped as he started to push into her, feeling her lips stretch and open as he pushed down on her perineum to be able to enter her. Once his head was inside her he slowly pushed in and out, his head glistening with her pussy juice … as Maria groaned "yes Xander now now" he pushed slowly but strongly into her, without pulling out. Maria was so wet for him his member slipped into her slowly and smoothly, she felt every single inch of him disappearing inside her, stretching her apart, entering her so deeply.

As he continued to enter her she felt her pussy expand yet again lengthways into her belly and felt again as if a giant's member was filling her so full. She felt him reach the end of her and push still further before she felt his full balls touch her ass and she knew she was fully filled. Xander did not pull out, he started moving side to side and around and around. He knew he was fully inside Maria, he felt every inch of her against his huge member. He groaned with desire and Maria grasped his butt cheeks and pulled them hard to her, forcing him to fill her deeper, if that were possible. He looked at her and they held eye contact as they were fully locked together, his huge engorged maleness completely filling between her legs; Maria's blue eyes stared into his dark brown ones and time stood still for them.

The electric energy between the two of them felt as if it was fusing them together and nothing else existed. He pulled out slightly and starting slowly rhythmically pumping into her, still looking into her eyes. Maria yet again was shocked at her own desire, she could literally have cum right then but she stopped herself. Then he pulled right out and played at her entrance, knowing it drove her wild; Maria could not help herself, she cried out as his huge head stroked her g-spot every time it pushed slightly in and out and she came around him, feeling his member harden as she came in shockwaves. Xander was so turned on, but he wanted to last a long time and he knew she wanted to cum with him when he finally filled her with his juice.

As her orgasm faded, he lay over her and started to suck her nipples again, while still moving his member inside her pussy. Maria told him to turn her over and he held her as he moved her on top of him so he lay on the bed, still inside her. Xander was strong and very athletic, and he loved the fact Maria was the same as he watched her, still keeping his huge member inside of her, move each of her legs up into a squatting position over him. She leant forward and supported her bent knees by resting them on her upper arms and held herself over him, taking some of her own weight on her hands. In this position she could raise her back up and down, letting her pussy ride up and down his hardness which was bolt upright under her.

"Maria OMG yes ... that is so good so good" Xander groaned under her, the feeling was incredible as he lay there, his cock rock hard up inside her as she moved.

She raised herself up so that just his throbbing head was inside her pussy and then rode up and down on it, feeling the lip of his head play with her lips every time it popped out then in again. She could see that this was driving Xander wild, she didn't want him to cum too soon so she slowly let her pussy move down and engulf his entire length, so she was sat on his hips, but his member completely up inside her. Then it was her turn to make slow circular movements, the feeling of being totally full of this Italian's enormous member was incredible. As she moved her hips, she felt her belly full of him, as his cock throbbed inside her, filling her.

Still joined together she leaned forward, dropped back onto her knees, seeking his mouth, and once again they kissed passionately on the lips, Xander moving his hips up and down to take her from underneath as she lay on top of him. Looking at her he licked his fingers, reached around and pushed one finger into her ass and felt her kiss him harder as he did so. He pumped up into her pussy, his finger pushing into her forbidden place at the same time.

"One day I want to take you here" he groaned, thrusting his finger into her ass.

"OMG yes Xander" she breathed.

Xander was imagining what it would feel like to take her pussy from behind then pull out and fill her ass with his hugeness and it turned him on unbelievably. But he did not want to do that now, it didn't feel right. Even though he knew he would probably not see her again after tonight.

Filled with desire he shifted down the bed under her, pulling abruptly out of her, then turned her over so she once again was lying on the bed under him. He moved down to her now gaping pussy with its engorged lips, and he was filled with primeval desire seeing how ready he had made her for him and how stretched she was by his member.

He licked her pussy lips, sucking on her clit as she begged him "Xander I want you, I want you so much, take me".

"You want me now Maria?" he said, his dark eyes boring into her.

"Yes now Xander fill me now" she begged.

He licked her pussy lips and flicked his tongue over her ass, then moved, once again grasping her ankles and spreading her legs wide for him. He knew he didn't need to be careful now, she was completely ready for him. As Maria breathed "now Xander now" he positioned his massive member at her entrance, her openness glistening pink and wet ready for him, her lips engorged … he then rammed his member fast and hard right up her, faster and harder than he had ever taken a woman before, she cried out as her pussy was totally filled up again, her body seemingly entirely full of him, she could not sense anything else except him. He pulled out fast, fully out and then on his knees between her legs he rammed into her again and again, Maria crying out every time he entered her. He pumped and pumped, full of a neanderthal desire to just take this woman, make her his one more time. There was a desperation to his powerful thrusting, this would be the last time, he thought as he rammed incessantly into her. As his member crashed into her lips, filling her pussy, again and again, he felt every inch inside her, feeling his orgasm building in the depths of him. He could not remember wanting to take someone this badly, he was totally oblivious to anything except this gorgeous woman and her pussy he was plundering … he was building and he wanted her to cum at the same time as him.

"Maria I am close" he gasped.

"Me too me too" she barely got the words out as she was holding her breath, making the sensation even stronger as she felt her final orgasm coming.

Xander let her ankles go and moved down over her body so that he was lying over her; Maria kept her legs in the air, stretching her thighs open as far as she could, allowing his hugeness to enter her fully. He was right over her face and licked her lips like an animal before crushing her in another kiss as he continued to violently pull out, pump in, pull out, pump in as hard as he could physically take her.

"You are mine you are mine" he groaned "I am gonna cum"

Maria held her breath as she felt the waves building up for her own orgasm. All she could feel was her pussy entirely stretched and pulsating, as this man was filling her hard, pumping her, filling her belly full of his huge hard weapon.

She sensed him now, close to orgasm and she opened her legs still further, feeling her stretched entrance and the inside of her pussy start to pulsate "take me take me" she cried out as he banged incessantly into her "yes Maria yes yes" he groaned in her ear "I am gonna give it to you" he heaved himself faster and faster into her as she started to cum, her whole body twitching and writhing under him.

"Yesssss" she let herself go and felt her pussy grasping at his member as he pumped hard into her one last time as he let his load shoot up into her. She felt the hot liquid hit the depths of her pussy as her orgasm twitched around his member and he thrust again and again deep into her, until he had cum completely. Their bodies, convulsing together with the aftershocks, finally became still.

Xander, already lying over Maria, then put his arms under her, right around her back and held her tightly to him.

"Maria" he breathed into her ear.

Maria kissed his neck which was sweatily hot, and she could feel his pulse, she could feel his heart beating against her breasts. She felt his chest quiver a little, but it was not an orgasm aftershock, she realised he was crying and it broke her heart. She couldn't help herself, she felt the tears sliding down her face. She felt so connected to this gorgeous man, what a whirlwind of emotions they had gone through together in just four days. You really couldn't make it up.

Xander, now the all-consuming desire had dissipated, had never felt so sad, so lonely or so scared, the emotions he had kept hidden for the last few weeks finally all burst to the surface at the same time. He convulsed with sobs and held Maria so tightly as if he didn't want her to ever get away. He didn't want to say goodbye to her and the knowledge of what the next day was going to bring suddenly hit him like a hammer. He felt like he could lose absolutely everything tomorrow, all at the same time. The boys, Maria and how were the girls going to accept him if they had never known him? How his boys were going to take the news he really didn't know. His ex, once she realised that he had not only had an affair but had gotten a woman pregnant long before he left her, would no doubt be out for blood and trying to influence the boys.

He just hoped they were old enough to be reasonable about it, once the inevitable initial shock wore off.

"Mi dispiace" he blurted out, into her neck.

"God Xander you have nothing to be sorry about" Maria said, kissing him again, she was well aware that a man like this was not used to crying, certainly not in front of anyone and especially a woman he had really only just met. She just held him, stroking his smooth muscular back. He was so gorgeous. The crazy idea that had germinated so suddenly earlier was now blossoming in her head, the logistics of it taking shape in the early hours of the morning as she asked herself what else she could do to help.

Eventually his member shrank and slithered out of her, followed by so much sperm Maria felt absolutely drenched. He rolled off her, but they lay close to each other, holding hands, for the next couple of hours, drifting in and out of a half sleep, until the alarm went off at 6am.

▲▲▲

CHAPTER EIGHT

▲

AU REVOIR

February 16

Xander got out of bed and went to his suite to pack his bag. Fortunately he had not really brought much to Paris with him, as he was not concentrating on his packing. At least, he thought thankfully, as he put all the signed papers in his case, the business side of this trip had gone perfectly. The client had signed a multi-million euro contract for the new office building. His flight to Florence was at 13.00, with check in from 11.30, so he decided to take Zeus to the Bois de Boulogne again quickly for a last proper walk before his long car journey. The freshness and solitude of the virtually empty forest at that time of day made him more clear-headed but none the less sombre. He was trying to decide how he would break the news to Gianni and Marco, what would he say?

How do you break news like that to your kids? With a nostalgic smile he played Canto della Terra at full blast on the way home through the empty streets. The early-rising Parisians who noticed him in his Italian plated Maserati waiting at traffic lights, on the return to the hotel, with Andrea Bocelli on his stereo, smiled to themselves at the handsome stereotypical Italian. They had no idea what their soon to be departing Italian visitor was going through, appearances could be so deceptive.

While he was out Maria got up and quickly called Charles to explain what was happening and to sort out some final details.

She showered and got dressed in jeans and a t-shirt while she waited for Xander to return.

***

Xander came back with Zeus, retrieved the dog's rug and bowl and went to say goodbye to Maria.

"Maria, I will be leaving soon" he said quietly "I want you to know that the last four days have been the most enjoyable for me for a VERY long time, but obviously this is goodbye" his voice tailed off.

"I have had the best time too" she smiled, slightly sadly "OK Xander you have my number, please let me know when you land and tell me you are OK?" Maria said to him "and let me know how the girls are, once you have been to the hospital. Then, only if you want to, let me know how the boys take the news".

"OK yes of course I will" Xander said.

Clearly, she didn't want to upset him any more than he already was, Xander thought, he had to man up and go and sort out the latest meltdown in his life and forget about Maria. Soon she would be heading back to NYC and would be back in her normal life; she probably had hundreds of admirers, and none of them would be the fathers of two small children who were still in primary school.

"OK I will send you a message and thank you for looking after Zeus until Charles can pick him up. You have a Great Dane for company all day, I am so sorry Maria. I hope you did not have special plans for today! Charles is going to arrive at my house sometime late on February 18 in Firenze, in two days' time, I gave him my address".

"Don't worry about Zeus Xander, I will take care of him for you, just go and do what you have to do back home OK" Maria said, moving towards him and putting her arms around his waist, her hands making their way up his muscular back.

Xander was dressed in jeans, sneakers and a white t-shirt and still looked drop dead gorgeous, despite the stress and tension visible on his face. They stood together, just holding each other for a long time, then Xander bent to kiss her mouth very gently and slowly. He drew back and looked at her intensely, his eyes glistening.

Maria had thought this guy could not get any more attractive but seeing his vulnerable side, how emotional he could get, just choked her up. Tears ran down her face as she looked at him and he reached up with his fingers and brushed them away.

"Maria listen to the lyrics of Canto della Terra" he said "I will always remember these unexpected days in Paris with you, goodbye Maria my bella ragazza".

"I will, and I will always remember this week Xander, goodbye" she smiled through her tears.

Once more lingering kiss and he turned quickly and left her suite, closing the door behind him.

**

Maria felt as if an emotional hurricane had come through her life. This was only her fifth day in Paris, but it felt as if she had been here at least two weeks already. Now she had a huge dog to look after until she could get him home to Italy ... and Xander had no idea what she was planning.

Charles had immediately agreed to take Xander to the airport but had confided to her he could not possibly leave Paris for two days. Although Maria had booked him for the entire week, he had family commitments tonight and tomorrow which meant the trip to Italy was impossible. Maria had known about these of course and had not made any plans to need the car during the evening anyway. Her crazy plan was already taking shape.

Maria would be driving the Maserati the approximately 1,400km back to Italy, with Lisette and her girls for company, plus Zeus in the back. OK so she had never driven in Europe before but how hard could it be. She had decided not to go through the Alps and via Milan, which was the shortest way, she wanted to go directly south, the entire length of France, to the Mediterranean then cross the border into Italy after stopping in Monaco. The Maserati had GPS, they would be fine. She had already quickly checked hotels and was planning to drive south to Lyon directly from the airport today. From there they would leave early the next day and drive to Monaco, staying at a four star hotel overlooking the sea, just on the border of France next to the Stade Louis II football stadium, which accepted dogs.

They had time for a quick afternoon/evening visit to Monaco and the famous Monte-Carlo before they then did the final leg of the journey through into Italy and over to Florence the next day, arriving on the evening of February 18. Then, she really hoped Xander would be pleased to see them all and have them to stay for a night. They would not outstay their welcome at what would be a very emotional time for Xander and his family. Lisette had already booked flights for all four of them from Florence to Venice Marco Polo airport the following afternoon, where they would spend a couple of days in Venezia before returning home to NYC together.

She checked her cell phone and found messages from Luisa, Carla, Lisette, Luke and Anna. The girls were absolutely hyper. They were used to exciting adventures with their Mom but this was the best yet. They had done several road trips together in the States but this was unknown territory. There was a message from Luke, wishing them a safe trip. Maria knew he had just starting dating one of the guys he trained. She hoped this one worked out, Luke was a really gorgeous guy, dark-skinned, with a body to die for, but he had not had anyone serious in his life for a long time. Anna's message just told her to take care and that she knew Maria was doing the right thing.

Lisette's message, which had arrived earlier in the morning, confirmed that all three of them were at JFK waiting to board imminently. They would already be in the air right now. She had found a flight so quickly, Maria was impressed but not surprised, the blonde bombshell had yet again proved her achieve-the-impossible reputation! Fortunately, Lisette already had a visa as she was working on the film set design in Marseille soon and the girls of course had Dutch passports. They would arrive at 14.00 Paris time at Charles de Gaulle airport north east of Paris.

Maria would leave the hotel soon, find somewhere near the airport to walk Zeus before their flight arrived, then pick them up directly from the terminal. Xander had no idea of course but his 13.00 flight would fly directly over her, she thought with a smile. She hoped her plan would please him, once they arrived in two days' time! Lord only knows what he would have gone through after the next 48 hours had elapsed. Once she had picked up Lisette, Luisa and

Carla from CDG she would head around the east of Paris through Créteil to pick up the A6 that would take them south towards Dijon then Lyon.

Maria quickly googled then booked a nice sounding hotel in Lyon for their night tonight. She had found one in the old part of the city, it used to be a convent and looked full of history. Looking at the awesome pictures on the website it was a shame they were not stopping long enough to look around the ancient city properly. They would have just a very brief taster of Lyon, France's third biggest city after Paris and Marseille, and its over 2000 years of history, before leaving for the South of France in the morning.

As she packed her things, she felt a buzz of excitement. She felt really alive. This was not at ALL what she had planned for this week, she had imagined a relaxing week in Paris of massages and museum visits, then the flight home in three days' time. Now instead of flying back to JFK, she would be arriving after a very long journey, in ITALY, in Florence, in someone else's Maserati, to deliver a dog back to his gorgeous owner. And Lisette and the girls were coming too! She knew Xander would be in the middle of an emotional nightmare when she got there but, selfishly, she was pleased she was going to get to see him again, one last time.

"OMG I honestly can't believe I am doing this" she said inwardly to herself, getting goosebumps.

She was waiting for Charles to come back from dropping Xander at the airport. The hotel knew that Charles was picking up Signor Sabatini's car. What they didn't know was that he would be loading Zeus into the car, driving it 200m down the road, where he would then hand it over to Maria. Then, very kindly, he had told Maria he would get back into his Mercedes that he had left in a side street, and drive it out to CDG, for the second time that morning, so that she could follow him out of Paris. Then, she was on her own.

The plan worked perfectly, Maria helped Charles get Zeus into the Maserati, then went back and checked out. She left the hotel on foot, politely refusing their offer to call a taxi.

"Merci beaucoup et au revoir » Maria smiled as she left, pulling her case behind her.

**

Around the corner, although she knew she had always had a very overactive imagination, Maria felt like she was in some action adventure film with the "secret meet". Charles put her case on the back seat and held the door of the Maserati open for her as she climbed into the driver's seat. He thanked her for the week, said he hoped everything would go well on the huge drive through Europe, then closed the door and went back to his Mercedes. He was full of admiration for the bravery of this nice American lady, and he hoped that this romance might work out for her and Signor Sabatini, they made a lovely couple.

Maria breathed in the Maserati's familiar leather mixed with Dior Sauvage scent and her stomach turned somersaults at the memory of him. As they pulled away and she started to follow Charles through all the now-familiar Parisian streets she told herself *"you will be careful, you will NOT damage this car!"* It felt so strange to be in the driver's seat.

She smiled slightly nervously to herself, gripped the leather steering wheel and took a deep breath … this was truly the start of a massive new road trip adventure.

▲▲▲

CHAPTER NINE

▲

LYON

February 16

Maria was glad she had followed Charles out of Paris. Even with a sat nav there was a lot of heavy traffic negotiating to do. After 30 minutes walking Zeus in an open grassy area near the airport watching overhead flights and wondering which one was headed to Florence with Xander on board, Maria checked the arrivals on her cell and saw the JFK flight was on time. She got Zeus, who seemed to be quite happy that she was taking care of him, back in the car and sat quietly for a moment, mentally going through the huge drive in front of her.

She thought she had better check the car had its documents, just in case, and looked in the glove box. It felt strange, as if she was invading Xander's privacy, as there were things in there clearly belonging to the boys. As she rummaged around looking for anything remotely related to the car, she found a photocopy of Xander's driving licence. As she picked it up to look at his photo, she noticed with a shocked, but not really surprised, smile that his date of birth was exactly the same as hers, March 25. Well, she thought, maybe that explains why we get on so well, and it is so fiery hot, we are both Aries and born on the same day, same year! How weird though, she thought with a sigh, remembering their unbelievable sexual chemistry. She put it back, closed the glove box and set off to pick up her daughters and Lisette at the airport.

Rather than park, she drove right to their terminal with the taxis and waited there. She figured that being American in an Italian car she could probably sweet talk the airport police if she was approached. She knew they had come through customs and excitedly looked out for her girls. There they were! With the unmistakeable tall blonde Lisette, all three pulling small suitcases. Maria had warned them there was not much space due to a horse taking up the entire trunk.

"Mom" came the shrieks.

"Mariiiiiaaaaa" from Lisette.

She hugged them all, even though she had only seen them for the last time six days ago, it felt like weeks, the amount of things that had gone on since they last saw each other.

"OMG it's so good to see you guys" Maria said, as they packed the cases into the middle of the back, Luisa and Carla one each side and Lisette in the front.

The girls immediately turned around to greet and stroke Zeus.

"OMG he is much bigger than Bella!" they both agreed as the Dane's large face sniffed them interestedly before lying back down and settling for a sleep.

"Whoah this car smells gooooood" Lisette immediately commented.

"That'll be the Maserati leather interior combined with Dior Sauvage" Maria said naughtily.

"OMG I like this guy already" said Lisette "and I hope his brother smells as good hahaha" she giggled.

Lisette was easily the loudest of Maria's friends, she was blonde (mostly natural), blue eyed, slim and had very large natural breasts that she was not shy of showing off. She attracted men like bees to a honey pot.

As soon as they were all in, Maria set off and left CDG. They had a long way to go, about four hours driving, and she didn't want to do too much driving in the dark the other end. She hoped they would get there at dusk if they were lucky. She was following the main roads around the east of Paris towards Créteil when they saw signs for INSEP, the elite French national sports training centre in the Bois de Vincennes.

"Oooh there's INSEP" said Lisette excitedly "that's where Tony Parker went" Lisette was seriously into basketball and the NBA, but even Maria knew that the retired San Antonio Spurs player was the most famous French basketballer.

"Oh this is so exciting" Lisette chirped "what's the Maserati like to drive?"

"Amazing" Maria said.

This was the first time she had ever driven one and the smooth driving experience was truly awesome. She was concentrating for the moment, watching out for where they were joining the A6, the busiest autoroute in France that linked Paris with the South of France via Lyon.

"OMG 460 km!" Luisa said from the back, Maria had turned onto the A6 "that sounds so far!" but as Carla pointed out the distances were in km and not miles and as they drove steadily south they noticed the total distance on the regular signage dropping more quickly than they expected.

They chatted about so many things they just ate up the miles without realising. After about three hours the city of Dijon was approaching.

"Hey land of the famous Maille mustard" Lisette commented as they passed the exit for Dijon.

Maria hoped Zeus would stay asleep, like Bella usually did in the car, for a long time, then they could stop fairly near Lyon for a snack and a walk stop. The French countryside was beautiful, and they all tried to take in as much of the view as possible.

Maria filled them in with more detail about what had happened to Xander and why they were taking the car back to Italy. They were all horrified at his shock discovery and then the accident which was obviously going to alter his life quite drastically, once the girls moved in.

Once Luisa and Carla were settled on watching series on their iPads in the back, Lisette then quizzed Maria about Xander.

"So, come on then, tell me everything" she said quietly "I want to know ALL the details".

"OMG Lisette it is totally crazy, it feels like I have known him forever, but I only saw him for the first time the day I arrived in Paris, which was only FOUR days ago!!"

When she said it out loud even Maria thought their story sounded fairly unbelievable.

"Yea so I saw him the following day at the Louvre and then we had dinner, then the day after, Valentine's, we had dinner again…" Maria glanced at Lisette and raised her eyebrows.

"Scale of 1-10?" Lisette asked.

"He is SO hot, honestly, about 250!!" Maria laughed "AND he has the same birthday as me can you believe it?"

"Jeeez Maria, it must be fate, men like that don't come around that often, I can't believe you were both in the same hotel!! And he has the same DOG!! It really is 101 Dalmations" Lisette laughed.

"Or rather, 101 Dalmations meets 50 Shades" she screamed with laughter.

"Then yesterday OMG Lise we went to this really cool museum and he was behaving a bit odd, then afterwards we went to this bar and after a tequila shot he told me about the little girls, he only found out about them just after Christmas, he met them three weeks ago for the first time, it's unreal" Maria said.

"The poor guy" Lisette said, "he must be stressed right out".

"That's an understatement" Maria said "you know I told you he thinks my driver I booked for the week, Charles, is bringing his car home, I didn't want to give him anything else to worry about. I just hope we can stay when we get there on the 18th, I got the impression he has quite a big villa outside Florence, but if the shit has hit the fan and it's awkward we can just go and find a hotel in Florence after we get there".

After more quizzing on the romantic side of things they then started discussing Monaco and then Venice and how exciting it was going to be to go there. They talked of canals, gondolas and St Mark's Square, it was so cool to be actually going to the famous ancient city.

The time passed surprisingly quickly and they stopped at an "aire", a rest stop, on the autoroute which had a café and plenty of wooded and grassy areas for Zeus. They got espresso from the machine and spent half an hour walking around under the trees with Zeus. It was dry and not as cold as Paris had been. Luisa and Carla were happy to play with Zeus and couldn't believe how much bigger he was than Bella, he was at least 20kg heavier and had legs like a horse!

Approaching Lyon the traffic was dense but Maria managed to navigate them through the endless lines of cars and trucks into the old part of the city, to the stunning villa hotel.

Once there, they left their bags in the rooms and went for a quick walk to stretch their legs around the old centre of Lyon, admiring the "twin" rivers that run through and merge in Lyon, the Rhône and the Saône. It was a very beautiful city with, they noticed, some really great boutiques although there was no time for any shopping! They walked around "Vieux Lyon" and admired the spot-lit basilica of Notre Dame de Fourvière up on the hill. As dusk fell Maria suddenly remembered what she should have been doing.

"Hey guys you know tonight, right now, I would have been at the top of the Eiffel Tower in Paris watching the lights come on all over the city!" she exclaimed "all alone, but here I am in Lyon, miles away from Paris, with you guys and on our way to Italy! How crazy is that!" They all laughed.

"Honestly Mom it's lucky we already had our party" the girls giggled.

"I hope the apartment is as I left it" Maria said with a half stern mom-voice.

They decided to have dinner in the hotel and get an early night, ready for their early start in the morning.

When Maria was lying in bed, unable to sleep, much later that night, her cell buzzed. It was a message from Xander. Her heart leapt when she saw it was a message from him. It was quite short, telling her he landed OK, he had been to the hospital and he was just with his family after telling the boys. They had taken the news OK but were pretty shocked. He hoped Maria had had a good day in Paris and he missed her.

"OMG" she thought to herself as she replied she was pleased for him and yes she was fine, and had had an exciting day. That was not a lie and luckily he did not ask any other questions about Paris. He must be busy with his family, she thought. He has no idea I am actually in a hotel in Lyon, with his dog! They exchanged a couple more raunchier texts and Xander mentioned their first night they had spent together and how he wished he had taken a photo of her in the underwear she had worn. Naughtily, Maria replied that actually she had taken some photos before she got dressed for dinner and waited for his reaction … "send me a photo" … she sent a couple of the very tasteful selfies she had taken before their Valentine's dinner date … and drifted off to sleep thinking about him.

**

In Italy that evening, Xander had just finished talking to Gianni and Marco. He had not had a relaxing flight at all. As he took off from CDG and the plane climbed over the eastern side of Paris, he had looked down at the city, thinking about Maria, he felt so close to her, they had a such a strong connection. As the plane had gathered height leaving Paris he had wondered if she was thinking about him too … what a shame he would never see her again, he really really liked her. Any more time with her, he thought, he could have fallen for her.

Antonio and Cristo and their kids were already at the villa, having a drink, waiting for Xander and the twins to come and talk with them. Xander's brothers had explained to their kids that they had two just recently-discovered cousins and had then told them the news that their uncle had received the night before. Chiara was telling her three girls the same news in Rome. Her three were probably the most excited, they were the youngest and didn't really grasp the seriousness of the situation, they were just looking forward to having cousins the same age to play with, instead of the five silly footballing boys who were much older than them and not at all interested in dolls or clothes. Virginia, their only girl cousin (until now) was great though, she was 17 and always played with them. They hoped Celestina and Alessandra would be OK and out of hospital soon "when can we go to Firenze and play?" they had asked.

Gianni and Marco were digesting the news. They had been shocked, of course, but had actually taken the news better than Xander expected. After the obvious question:

"Papa you really didn't know about them before? You have not been visiting them secretly all these years?"

To which Xander told them the truth, that he only found out six weeks before and had visited them just the once, three weeks ago.

Xander thought that if he had known all these years but not told them, that they would probably have gotten really angry at him and possibly not spoken to him for a long time, possibly never forgiven him. He would have understood that. Even though their existence was a shock, at least he was almost in the same boat as his boys, with this new life they were about to embark on. The only thing Gianni and Marco had been resentful of was the fact that he had cheated on their mama all those years ago, but with most of their friends also having divorced parents, for numerous reasons, they were not too shocked. They adored their papa and knew how much he had done for them over the years. Now they were older they understood what a nightmare they had been when they were younger and were a bit more accepting of other people's mistakes.

Xander was relieved that at last everyone knew, it was not a secret anymore, now they just had to deal with the situation and make plans for the girls to come home from the hospital to the villa. Luckily his home had plenty of bedrooms, it was a ten-bedroom villa with large gardens on a hill just outside Firenze. He would choose two rooms next to each other and quickly decorate them before the girls got home, he decided. He needed to buy lots of cuddly toys, pink ones, maybe unicorns, what else did little girls like? He would have to ask Chiara for help, he had never decorated bedrooms for girls before. He didn't know how things would go with regard to all their things in their mother's house. Maybe he should buy some clothes for them in case he had to wait before being allowed to take their things. Antonio was helping him sort out that side of it with a friend of his who was a lawyer. His thoughts drifted again to Maria for about the 1000th time since he had left Paris; he wondered how she had decorated her girls' bedrooms, when they were young in NYC. He bet she would have been very creative and made pretty bedrooms for them.

He told himself crossly yet again to stop thinking about Maria and went into the kitchen to pour himself a large glass of Chianti before taking the bottle and going out to join the others in the huge lounge with vaulted ceiling he had designed himself when he had the villa built. As he finished the glass of wine he took out his cell and texted Maria … then after the text conversation had turned sexy and she sent him the photos … he felt totally intoxicated and wasn't sure if it was the effect she had on him or the wine. He poured himself another glass and flicked through the photos again. She was so stunning, so sexy, he wished he could have spent longer with her.

Xander and his brothers consumed a lot of Chianti that night, the boys and Virginia drank beer. They all stayed up late. He had decided they must make these new family plans together and wanted everyone's input.

▲▲▲

CHAPTER TEN

▲

MONACO

February 17

After a delicious but early breakfast, Maria, Lisette and the girls checked out, loaded Zeus and drove out of Lyon. They had another huge journey ahead of them, approximately six hours including a couple of stops before they got to the next hotel just on the border of Monaco. They checked the route and saw that they would head directly south from Lyon, past places with very exotic names like Avignon, Aix-en-Provence and the famous Saint-Tropez, before arriving in Monaco mid-afternoon.

Once again, the time flew past, the Maserati easily eating up the kilometres as they drove further and further south towards the Côte d'Azur. As they got their first glimpse of the sea, although it was only February, they could see why it was called the "azure (blue) coast". The Mediterranean Sea was a clear turquoise blue.

The girls squealed from the back as they saw signs for Cannes. They followed a bunch of celebrities and influencers on Instagram and YouTube and many of them had been photographed there during the Cannes film festival.

"Mom can we go there, that's where the red carpet steps are, pleeeeease" they begged.

Maria dropped down off the autoroute and they wound their way down through Cannes right to the harbour, stopping outside the Palais des Festivals et des Congrès de Cannes where the film festival was held every year. They took photos quickly of each other posing on the iconic steps, before heading off again.

They decided, as they were now down on the coast, to drive through to Antibes then on to Nice but on the coast road instead of re-joining the motorway. It would take a little bit longer but the road should take them right to their hotel once they reached the border with Monaco, Maria figured, looking at the map. It was a good decision, the traffic was minimal, although they could well imagine what it would be like in the summer.

They drove slowly, making the most of the views. After they had driven around the long Promenade des Anglais through Nice, the road started to climb up from sea level and wound its way around the cliffs. This was where the route got truly stunning. They stopped a few times to take photos, the views of the bays with white yachts at anchor, sandy beaches and the turquoise sea were absolutely amazing. It looked hot enough to swim, but probably wasn't at this time of year.

As they drove the coast road Maria put the stereo on and they listened to Canto della Terra at full blast. Andrea Bocelli's exceptional voice was the perfect accompaniment to the beautiful landscape they were passing through, with its stunning cliffs, pine trees and picturesque bays.

They arrived at the hotel, parked in the underground car park next to all the Bentleys and Ferraris, then after checking in, took Zeus around the cliff path for a walk before settling him in the room. They had a great view over the marina in front of the hotel, with the Mediterranean Sea behind it. They could see the helicopter shuttle flights, regularly flying between Nice airport and a helipad just behind the marina.

They had time for a late afternoon visit so they took the hotel shuttle bus the short distance over the border (which was over the road outside the hotel!), past the Stade Louis II and into Monaco itself. The driver dropped them in Monte-Carlo where they saw the famous casino and walked around the designer shops. Monaco was beautiful, so clean and with perfectly manicured gardens. They walked back down to the main harbour and admired the huge yachts moored there, before walking up to "The Rock" headland where the royal palace was located. The streets up there were so quaint and the views out over the sea from the exquisite gardens were just breathtaking. They went briefly into the beautiful cathedral and saw the tombs of Prince Rainier and Princess Grace Kelly.

Dinner that night in the hotel was amazing, the girls decided to order "truffle burgers" which turned out to be burgers but the meat was mixed with the expensive truffles (type of fungi) that are sniffed out by dogs under oak trees. They were totally delicious. Maria and Lisette had grilled cod on a sublime mashed potato with fresh vegetables. They stayed in the bar and had a cocktail, all excitedly chatting about everything they had seen, before getting an early night.

The next day Maria knew they had to head east, leaving the Principality of Monaco, go back into France briefly past the very beautiful town of Menton, then cross over the Italian border and follow the autostrada. They would go past Genoa, continue down the Italian coast, then she planned to stop at Pisa for lunch. They could not go so close to that city and NOT see the famous leaning tower! Then, they would be on schedule for Charles's original arrival time outside Florence early evening at the villa. *"OMG what a trip"* Maria thought to herself again, she really hoped Xander would be pleased to see them all, she was getting a bit nervous about when they actually arrived. Paris and the time she had spent with Xander already seemed very far away and the end of this colossal journey was not that far off.

**

Xander messaged again that night, telling Maria he had been to the hospital, the girls had been very upset and that he missed her again. Maria replied she missed him too and didn't mention anything to do with Paris. They didn't talk for long and she fell asleep easily that night, the driving was catching up with her. It was a shame Lisette didn't have a driving licence, as Maria had to do it all herself. Lucky she had such an awesome car to drive, she told herself!

**

That night, in the villa outside Florence, things were slightly calmer than the night before, although the wine glasses were still constantly being re-filled and everyone was still digesting the new family news. The twins in hospital were recovering, Xander had been to see them that morning and thankfully they had seemed pleased to see him. The doctors had explained to them, while he was there, about their mama. Xander had given them cuddles as they cried, wanting their mama back. They looked so lost and forlorn. Xander had told them about their big brothers, all their cousins and how everyone could not wait to meet them and look after them. He didn't know what else to say to them, but they had seemed to accept what he was saying. Chiara had arrived from Rome with her three girls, but her husband Roberto di Arellano was working so he had stayed in the capital. Of all the four siblings Chiara was the only one who seemed to have found happiness in her marriage. Antonio had admitted he was having problems, which was why his wife wasn't there. Xander and Cristo were already divorced.

The three youngest cousins, Isabella, Marina and Gabriella, were super proud and excited as Chiara had told them on the journey up from Roma that their "Zio Xan" wanted them to help buy toys, princess clothes, beds and other girly things as their uncle had no idea what to get.

Xander had decided to decorate one room instead of two, thinking that the poor girls would probably want to sleep together. They could always do a second room in the future. The shock was wearing off slightly, being replaced by his paternal need to protect them, the same way he had always protected his boys.

The girls were going shopping the next day in Firenze but had to be back before the evening as the giant Zeus was going to be arriving home with a private CHAUFFEUR! They thought this was highly amusing, they loved Zio Xan's dog.

Xander texted Maria briefly. He missed her but didn't really know what to say, he knew she would be leaving for the States the day after tomorrow. He had plenty to concentrate on, he needed to forget her, but it was proving easier said than done.

▲▲▲

CHAPTER ELEVEN

▲

ZEUS ARRIVES HOME

February 18

Cristofano Sabatini was outside Xander's villa, having yet another cigarette, when he saw the black Maserati approaching from a distance up the country road towards the drive to the villa. He had taken up smoking again since his divorce, although he was very fit and went to the gym most days. He looked like Xander, tall and muscular but less angular in his facial features, with shorter dark hair. Xan and Antonio called him the "pretty one" which although was a compliment he wasn't sure if he liked being called pretty and anyway Antonio was the one who had done some modelling when he was younger. Cristo was lively, and prone to emotional outbursts, much more so than his siblings. Their parents always said he took after his paternal grandfather from Naples who had been a boxer with a horrible temper.

The villa was on a hill outside Firenze in the most beautiful countryside, the open country roads lined with tall cypress trees in quintessential Tuscan style. His poor brother, he thought, taking a long draw on his cigarette, the news he had told them just after Christmas had been shocking, but hey these things happen to guys. Lord knows how many kids are on the planet whose fathers don't even know they exist. Then there are the poor bastards who are lied to and tricked into paying for kids they didn't plan. You don't think it is going to happen to *you*, but it happens.

So up until two days ago he, Xan and Antonio had been working out when to tell all the kids about their new sisters/cousins. Of course this accident had accelerated everything. Antonio had called Chiara in Rome the next day to tell her, as Xander had been planning to visit her next week and tell her in person then. She had taken it pretty well, she was a cool sister, she just felt really sorry for Xan and wanted to know if she could help with the girls once they came home from the hospital. Her three girls were 6, 8 and 10 so they would be happy with two surprise girl cousins! Chiara had been more worried about how Xan's ex was going to take the news, none of them had ever liked her very much and although Gianni and Marco would probably calm down and accept it quite quickly, their mother was unpredictable. Nobody envied Xan the first conversation with her.

Xan had told them that the Maserati would be arriving today early evening, driven by an ex-military chauffeur aged about 55, called Charles, who was French. As Cristo watched the car turn and come up the drive he frowned as he caught sight of the driver. That certainly wasn't Charles, whoever the hell he was, and the passenger (Xan had not mentioned any passengers) was very blonde and very female! The driver was also clearly a woman, a pretty one. He walked towards the car as it approached and could see the rear seat had passengers too. What the fuck was going on.

Cristo was tired and not in the mood for any more nasty surprises, they had enough to deal with already. They hadn't gotten much sleep since Xan got back two days ago and they had drunk a lot of red wine while deciding on a plan of action. He took another long draw on his cigarette and felt his simmering annoyance go up a notch. He was in the sort of mood that when he was younger had usually meant he went out drinking and got into a fight.

The Maserati slowed on the crunchy gravel and stopped on one side of the huge olive tree in a big raised bed that created a sort of "roundabout" in front of the villa. Cristo extinguished then threw his cigarette into a flower bed (yes he knew Xan hated him doing that) and walked onto the drive towards the car as all the doors opened at once.

"What the fuck …" he said under his breath. It was Xander's car but it had certainly not returned from Paris with some ex-military chauffeur! He could not believe his eyes as first a stunning brunette stepped out of the driver's side, then the most gorgeous tall blonde woman he had ever seen got out of the passenger side, smiling widely at him! The driver hadn't seen him and had gone straight around to the trunk, Cristo assumed Zeus was in there, or he hoped he was, as the blonde, wearing jeans and a low cut red t-shirt which did nothing to hide her ample breasts came towards him. Cristo's eyes widened.

Lisette's first thought on seeing the guy who must be Xander was *"lucky bitch"*, he was cute, way cuter than Maria had described! She had imagined someone with a hooked nose and stronger chin after her description of his angular features. This guy looked like a model.

"Hey" she smiled and said in her American accent "you must be Xander? Maria told me you speak English, sorry I don't speak

Italian, I'm Lisette" she smiled, tipping her head to one side, her blonde hair moving in the light breeze.

"Buongiorno" said Cristo, moodily, "I speak a little English yes, but my name is Cristofano, I am Xander's brother" his dark eyes bored into her.

"Oh, oh OK, sorry, erm ... it is nice to meet you" Lisette stared at him with her clear blue eyes as she tried to speak clearly for him. He was absolutely gorgeous, Lisette told herself to calm the fuck down, this was not at ALL the moment to be checking out guys, but she gave him a huge smile. Cristo didn't smile but his annoyed mood had immediately lifted, giving way to mildly carnal curiosity.

Another gorgeous guy and a pretty dark-haired woman came out of the villa and Lisette worked out this must probably be the other brother and Xander's sister. Antonio was also smoking, he looked brooding, staring at the new arrivals. Chiara was intrigued, who on earth was the blonde and who were the other people, who had all arrived in Xan's Maserati! She thought some guy was bringing the car back with Zeus.

"OK d'accordo but who are you?" Cristo asked, as Zeus leapt out of the car, barking, and two pretty young teenagers approached with the brunette who had been driving. They all looked at each other, and Maria started to explain.

**

Xander's head was aching, he was in the back of the villa in the kitchen making yet another coffee when he heard barking.

"Zeus my boy" he said, smiling to himself, realising Charles must have arrived, he had made quite good time considering he was driving alone as it was only 5pm. He quickly made his way out of the kitchen to the back terrace that looked out over a stunning view of the Tuscan countryside and came around the front of the villa from the side, bending down to greet Zeus who was jumping and wagging in sheer delight at seeing his master, panting and slobbering everywhere. Only then did he look up to greet Charles in the driveway. Antonio, Cristo and Chiara were already there talking to someone.

As he stood up Xander caught his breath *"what the ..."* it was Maria!! He felt the hair stand up on his arms as disbelief then excitement ran like lightning bolts through his body. What on earth was she doing here? She should be in Paris, it was her last night tonight before she flew home tomorrow! And who were the other people? And where was Charles?

Maria had introduced herself to the others and explained very quickly that Charles had not been able to make the drive and that she had brought Zeus home. Cristo was gobsmacked, this must be the woman Xan had met in Paris, who was still in Paris, except she wasn't, she was here. She and the others must have travelled, he reckoned, about 1500km and for at least two days to get here by car, he thought. Chiara also realised instantly who she must be and was immediately impressed at this lady's calm attitude after what must have been a colossal journey halfway across Europe. She was very beautiful too, Xander had not been exaggerating.

Maria walked over and approached Xander slightly hesitantly, she was suddenly feeling shaky, he was waiting at the edge of the driveway circle, still being assaulted by Zeus, but he was staring at her in disbelief.

"Ciao Xander" she said softly "Charles couldn't make it, so I brought Zeus back home for you". She held out his Maserati keys, smiling at him, although she was trembling. She really was not sure how he was going to take this turn of events, or what he had been going through since she last saw him, she wondered if the apprehension was showing in her eyes.

Xander had thought that the emotional tidal waves were abating, but this? He literally could not believe that Maria, who he had left in her suite in Paris two days ago, never to be seen again, was standing in front of him outside his own villa!!

"Maria sei qui ... what, how?" he just blurted out and took her into his arms, holding her to him tightly, before releasing her but holding her arms and staring at her again "what are you doing here, you are in Paris!?"

Maria started to tell him all at once about Charles not being able to leave Paris, how she had realised she herself could take Zeus home, how she had had the crazy idea that Lisette and her daughters could come and keep her company on the drive, meeting them from CDG the same afternoon Xander left, Lyon, then Monaco, all the driving ... now they had finally arrived, she had done it, she suddenly felt very tired and emotional now she was really in Italy and Xander was standing right in front of her ... her eyes started to fill with tears.

"Don't worry Xander we are not all staying, we know you have enough to deal with, we can find a hotel in Florence" she babbled, as a tear escaped down her cheek.

"Come here Maria" he kissed away her tears. He could not believe she had driven his car all the thousands of kilometres from Paris in northern France, with his dog, all the stops she must have made for him. Where had they stayed? He folded her into his arms.

"You will all stay here, at least for tonight, how can I thank you enough, I cannot believe it, I thought I would never see you again, I can't believe you are here" … and holding her face he kissed her softly on the mouth then held her tight, oblivious to the crowd of people who were now on the driveway, as Gianni and Marco and their cousins had joined everyone busily greeting the newly arrived strangers.

**

Zeus was sniffing around, running between his family and his new friends, as Luisa and Carla went to get his things from the trunk. They came back to the group with Zeus's bowl, rug and food and looked shyly at the group of boys and girls all speaking in Italian, wondering which of them actually lived here.

Marco saw they didn't know who to give Zeus's things to, so he stepped forward and introduced himself in broken English.

"I do not speak very well English" he said "give me the things, thank you, grazie tanto"

"Marco!" Antonio spoke in rapid Italian "can all of you take the girls into the villa and see if they want a drink, you can use the games room". The games room at the villa was in the basement and had its own bar, table football, pool table and lounge area with cinema seating for the large TV screen. Xander had installed an expensive Bose stereo system and they had had many parties down there over the years.

"Come with me" Marco said, so Luisa and Carla, followed by all the others, who were very interested in the new and very unexpected arrivals, made their way into the house. In the last two days all their lives had changed with the fairly shocking news they had received. Now these American visitors were here as well. It was like life had decided to insert a huge blip in their normally routine existence of studies, friends and social life.

The youngest girls were confused and kept asking in very cute sounding Italian voices "Who are they? Who are the ladies? Why did Zeus come with them? Why was the lady driving Zio Xan's car?". They thought the girls were very pretty, and had funny voices, they didn't understand anything they said. Their cousins told them they were American and they should practise their English on them. Gianni joked with Isabella, the oldest of them, who was ten …

"Come on Isa I know you learn English at school, say something" he said in Italian, poking her arm.

"My name is Isabella and I am from Italy" she squeaked perfectly.

"Oh that is sooooo cute" Luisa and Carla exclaimed both together, smiling widely.

"Mi chiamo Luisa" Luisa said.

« E mi chiamo Carla" said Carla. They had been practising very basic Italian in the car for the last two days, they wished they knew more now. Everyone seemed really nice.

The three little girls laughed, delighted, and tried to teach them other things. They took to Luisa and Carla very quickly and asked them something they did not understand at all. Alberto, Antonio's son translated:

"They say they really want to meet their new cousins, they say do you want to see the bedroom the new twins are going to sleep in?"

The little girls were desperate to show even more people all the special things they had helped buy for the poor twins who had lost their mama, who were coming to live here, with Gianni and Marco. They agreed to go and have a look later, for now they all settled themselves in the sofa area of the games room, all hesitantly smiling at each other. The basement games room was so cool Luisa and Carla thought, really fun. They noticed a second TV screen the other end, with gaming chairs set up in front of it. Teenagers' heaven, Xander called it.

"Would you like some coffee or juice" Marco asked them, pronouncing it "jooz".

The girls smiled and asked for a glass of water and an orange juice, before sitting down to be officially introduced to everybody, as there were nine of them altogether. Gianni, apart from being obviously identical to Marco except for slightly longer hair, seemed to be a bit shyer. The girls could not believe how much they both looked like Matteo Bocelli, their mom had been right (the fact that mom actually knew who he was was quite impressive, she was cool, as moms go). The boys introduced them to their cousins Giovanni and Pietro (known as Piero) who were Cristo's boys, Alberto and Virginia, then the three younger girls Isabella, Marina and Gabriella. Antonio's daughter Virginia was 17 and came over and sat with them, smiling and trying to explain in her school-learnt English what a surprise it was to see them! She tried to explain that her uncle told them "a man" was bringing Zeus back to Italy not four girls! They all laughed.

The boys were really friendly and Marco explained that it was "a bit difficult" at the moment but everyone was trying to get things ready for the twins who were in hospital (he didn't say "our sisters") but coming to live here in a couple of days. Gianni just half smiled as his brother explained, his dark eyes slightly guarded behind his flop of dark hair, he always let Marco do the talking.

Luisa and Carla told them they knew what had happened as their mom had met their papa in Paris and that was why they had come all the way from NYC, to help bring their dog back. The boys were impressed at this and asked a lot of questions about New York. They wanted to know if the girls had been to Madison Square Garden and seen the New York Knicks. When they found out they had been to a lot of the home matches they thought it was cool, even though the girls explained that well, they lived in NYC and supported the Knicks. They put on some music and they all tried to chat, which got very amusing with the language barrier.

▲▲▲

CHAPTER TWELVE

▲

THE VILLA

February 18

Outside on the drive Cristo was not doing a very good job of trying not to show how gorgeous he thought Lisette was. Lisette herself was not making a huge effort to hide her immediate attraction for him. She always said flirting was her natural state of being. Cristo invited her for a tour of the villa gardens and they disappeared together. Antonio and Chiara made their way back into house leaving Xander and Maria outside together.

"Come with me" Xander said to Maria, taking her hand.

He led her back down the drive and across to where the gardens looked out over a steep hill; you could see the city of Florence in the distance and the distinctive roof of the cathedral Santa Maria del

Fiore or Il Duomo as it was commonly known. The view was truly breathtaking.

"You live in a very beautiful place Xander" Maria said, turning to him.

"Maria I still cannot believe you are here, how you got here!" he exclaimed, putting his arms around her waist and staring at her "this should be your last night in Paris! And you were going to go up the Eiffel Tower after I left!"

"I know right, I still can't believe it myself" she laughed.

Now the worry of how he might react had dissipated she was just so happy to be here "I didn't plan to come to Italy this trip, we even saw the leaning tower of Pisa at lunchtime!" she looked up at him, at his familiar dark angular features, his aquiline nose and sensual full lips.

"I am so glad I chose this week to go to Paris on business" Xander said, looking at her seriously "originally I was going to go this coming week but I brought it forward. But they say there is no such thing as coincidence" …

"So am I" Maria smiled "it made my week much more exciting than I planned!" then, she quickly added "oh I am so sorry Xander that was thoughtless, how have you been, these last two days?"

"Gianni and Marco have been great" Xander said and he proceeded to tell her about how he told them, their reaction and what the family had planned "it's lucky I have a lot of bedrooms" he smiled "my whole family is here at the moment".

He explained that Maria, Lisette and the girls could stay in the guest wing, which had two bedrooms and a lounge area. He and his family were shared between seven other bedrooms, with the tenth one being the one that was about to be quickly decorated, starting tomorrow.

"The guest wing is close to my master bedroom" Xander added naughtily, putting his hands to her face and kissing her passionately "but of course you must be very tired after the journey from Monaco today"

"Well after that drive my whole body is aching, what I really need is a massage ..." she said, laughing.

"I will give you a long massage later" Xander murmured into her ear "after you have relaxed with me in my jacuzzi in my en suite, with a glass of champagne of course, it is the least I can do for you after you drove across Europe to deliver a dog"

"That sounds perfect Xander" Maria said, kissing his neck, over his shoulder she could see the Tuscan countryside rolling away in an endless vista of beautiful hillsides, this place was so romantic.

At her touch he felt his body immediately harden with the familiar desire. The desire he had had for her ever since he first laid eyes on her in the lobby of the hotel. Which, crazily, was only six days ago. He put his arms around her forcefully and pulled her to him, kissing her on the lips hard, before moving his hands to her face and holding her as he thrust his tongue into her mouth and they kissed passionately. They stayed like that for a long time, kissing as if they had been given borrowed time together and there was not a moment to lose. The sexual chemistry between them was, if possible, stronger than it had been in Paris. The emotions and what they had both gone through in the last two days since they last saw each other added to the already electric charge between them. She could feel his hardness in his trousers, pressing urgently against her and she felt herself moisten at the memory of the last night they had spent together in her suite.

"Let me give you a tour of the villa would you like that?" he said, finally pulling away from her, breathless, gazing at her, the sexual desire making his brown eyes darken to near-black.

"That would be great" Maria said, reaching for his hand, she couldn't wait to see where he lived, the villa and gardens he had designed and built.

Xander told her the villa was called Villa Volterra, which was also the name of a town not far away. Maria thought the name sounded oddly familiar, from a long time ago, but she must have seen it on road signs as they drove here earlier today, she supposed. He explained that the very ancient town of Volterra still had the remains of its original Etruscan walls and was famous for the alabaster mined there.

Xander took her around the edge of his property, past where the ground stepped down slightly and he had several stone statues dotted between raised beds of beautiful shrubs. They walked around the lower limit of his gardens along a slabbed path, admiring the established trees and the view through them across the countryside, before making their way further around to the back of villa. The villa itself was a two storey classic Italian building with a terracotta tiled roof, straight out of one of those "learn to paint in Tuscany" holiday brochures. It was stunning. Maria could see two balconies, one at either end and Xander told her one of them was his private balcony. As she looked at the stone balustrade around the balcony, she had a sudden erotic vision of being taken by Xander from behind, as she was leaning on the balustrade wearing a silk negligée in the early morning, with mist in the valleys. She reached for his hand and they glanced at each other, their eyes full of desire.

There was a small fountain and pool, with water pouring out of stone urns held by angels. The pool, which could be seen from the back terrace of the villa, Xander explained was surrounded in the summer by blue and dark purple irises and blue agapanthus. There were enormous amethysts set each side of the water cascades, and the purple crystals gleamed. Without thinking she reached for the tanzanite pendant she was wearing, that she had bought in Paris. She had always been drawn to the purple gemstone.

"Your necklace is very beautiful" Xander said as he turned her to him, touching the tanzanite, "like you my bella Maria".

They stayed there for a moment, the design was just beautiful and Maria told Xander how lovely she thought it all was. When the flowers were out it would look stunning. Xander was so pleased she liked it, he had spent a long time designing the gardens and he did a lot of the gardening himself. Cutting the grass in summer was a pleasure but took him hours to finish if he did it himself. He employed a gardener from the local village who came three days a week from March to October. Maria could imagine when the weather was better Xander and his boys must spend a lot of time on the terrace, just enjoying the gardens and this view. The girls would now too, of course, she remembered, thinking of the twins in the hospital.

As they came around to the part of the gardens that were to the side of the villa, Maria could hear squawking, but not the sound of normal wild European birds, definitely exotic.

"Do you keep birds Xander?" she asked, intuitively knowing what he was going to say, she could already see them in her mind's eye … how did she know … she sensed them.

"Oh yes I have eight blue macaws, they are very noisy sometimes" Xander said with a smile "do you like birds Maria?"

Maria literally could not believe what he was saying and stared at him as she said "Xander I adore birds, and do you know what my favourite bird has always been, ever since I can remember?"

"Nooo …" he said with a smile "really?"

"Yup, blue macaws!" Maria said, shaking her head in disbelief, suddenly hoping they could hold them and touch their feathers. Once, on holiday in Mexico, she had held four macaws and had her picture taken with them. She remembered loving the feel of their feathers as she had been able to stroke their blue backs and wings.

"I guess we are not really surprised" Xander said smiling, drawing her to him and kissing her.

As they approached the aviary, which was enormous, and set fairly far back from the villa (so you could hear the sound of distant exotic bird calls and not just the crazy loud squawking they did sometimes, Xander joked) Maria could see them, perched on the various large branches of the trees inside their aviary.

"Do you want to see them before we go inside and have some drinks?" Xander asked, the unmistakeable smell of cooking lasagne was coming across from the kitchen.

"OMG that would be amazing" Maria said "whatever Chiara is cooking smells delicious".

"Oh that will be Antonio cooking, he loves it" Xander smiled. Maria remembered how Luke loved cooking and hoped things were working out with his new guy back in NYC.

They spent ten minutes inside the aviary, where Xander called a couple of the birds over. She watched Xander's hawk-like features as he "talked" to them and admired how such a big guy was so gentle with the birds. They had been babies last year, he explained, and were used to people, letting one hop onto Maria. As Maria stared at the huge bird on her arm and stroked its beautiful blue feathered back, she felt so happy. She looked at Xander and he was staring at her. The desire he felt for her was so strong it shocked him with its intensity, but he was not trying to deny his feelings to himself anymore, as he had done in Paris. When he left two days ago he had tried to accept she was going back to NYC and he would obviously never see her again. But now, seeing her here, and after the distance she had travelled across Europe to bring Zeus home to him…. he couldn't believe she was at his villa. The thought made him very happy. He didn't want her to leave. He wondered what on earth the four of them were planning to do, now they had brought Zeus back. They must be returning to NYC at some point. He would ask her later.

Further around, behind a stone wall and with another stunning view, Xander quickly showed her the swimming pool which was battened down for winter. Maria could just imagine how gorgeous it would be in summer. There was a large stone patio area with space for various sun loungers, an outdoor shower and a covered outdoor bar area. There were palm trees safely wrapped in their insulated "winter coats" in large pots at the edge of the stone-slabbed area and Maria could see spotlights. It would be stunning during the hot Tuscan nights, she thought.

As they came back towards the house Cristo and Lisette were approaching from the direction of the fountain pool. They were laughing and joking in a conspiratorial sort of way and Maria immediately recognised the predatory body language Lise the man magnet was using. Lise could never be called shy, that was for sure. They were walking very close together and were clearly attracted to each other. Cristo kept touching her arm as they spoke. Lisette's low-cut red t-shirt was clingy, her breasts bobbing as she walked. Xander noticed with mild amusement that Cristo's black mood which had been brewing for a couple of days seemed to have lifted.

"Hey Xander these ladies look thirsty I think it is time for a pre-dinner drink" Cristo said in Italian to his brother, smiling at Lisette, who had absolutely no idea what he just said, but it was in Italian and came out of Cristo's mouth, and was therefore incredibly sexy.

They set off back towards the house, Cristo talking to Xander in rapid Italian, glancing back a couple of times at them. Maria and Lisette exchanged glances.

"Maria, I think we should stay and visit Florence not Venice" she giggled, knowing full well they had flights booked the following afternoon "Cristo is gorgeous, I just about understand him" she laughed. Cristo turned round to look at her, hearing his name, and gave her a smouldering look.

Lisette looked back at Maria, widened her eyes and mouthed "OMG".

Maria laughed and they followed Xander and Cristo up to the villa and across the large stone terrace. There were various palm trees in huge terracotta pots, also wrapped with insulating coats, with oleanders and lavender in the flower beds. Xander explained that in summer they had a wooden table and chairs for outdoor eating and some outdoor sofas and armchairs. What a paradise this was, Maria thought. She loved her NYC apartment, which was spacious, but she wasn't used to this enormous amount of space.

The kitchen was large, with huge windows plus a patio door to the terrace, overlooking the most beautiful Tuscan view. Although it was February you could easily picture the view in summer. There was an open plan breakfast room at one end of the kitchen space, next to another set of patio doors, with the table laid for dinner.

Xander opened the doors and put his arm around Maria's waist as she stepped into the kitchen. At his touch she felt the same familiar jolt of electricity straight to the core of her being. They looked into each other's eyes and Maria just melted inside. Remember there are other guests here, she reminded herself, although Xander was not trying to hide his clear desire for her. Cristo took Lisette straight to the central island in the kitchen where Antonio and Chiara were chatting and poured her a large glass of red wine.

"Hey bro, we have taken the girls' luggage to the guest wing, I guess you wanted them to stay there?" Antonio smiled. He looked more relaxed than he had earlier and Xander hoped he had been talking to Chiara about whatever it was that had been bothering him since he arrived. Both Antonio and Chiara smiled at Maria, they seemed such nice people. Zeus was lying in the way, right in the middle of the kitchen floor, just like Bella always did.

"Xan I've got a lasagne nearly ready in the oven, the kids can eat first, then I'll cook ours" Antonio said.

Maria could smell the gorgeous aroma and saw another huge lasagne ready prepared for cooking waiting on the large hob. She bet his restaurant must be something else, she wondered where it was exactly in Florence. Chiara had made two large bowls of salad. Xander's kitchen had very large grey textured floor tiles, pale oak cupboards and all the work surfaces were dark grey speckled marble, it was stunning. All the walls were white and Maria smiled to herself as she noticed a set of three blue macaw prints in beautiful frames.

"Grazie Toni" Xander said, then, turning to Maria "would you like me to show you the villa and where you will be staying tonight?"

Maria glanced at Lisette who smirked cheekily at her and said "you guys go ahead, we are just chatting here, I'll come up and change in a minute".

Xander led Maria into a large corridor and showed her the enormous luxurious main lounge and a beautiful dining room "but we usually eat in the breakfast room if we are just family" he explained. There were various classy black and white photos of the boys and family photos on the walls.

They could hear happy sounds emanating from the basement from the group of kids and it sounded as if everyone was having a good time, if the volume of noise and laughter was anything to go by. Gabriella came running up the stairs and charged past them towards the kitchen, shouting at Xander in Italian as she went past. Xander laughed and looked pleased and Maria asked him what she had said.

"She said please please pleeeeeeease can the American girls stay with us for longer, we love them" Xander laughed, then added "that actually sounds like a great idea to me" staring at Maria with his intense dark eyes.

Maria smiled at him and took his hand. He had already told her during their walk in the garden that he was going to visit the twins in hospital in the morning.

"Xander that does sound like a very tempting idea" she paused and stared back at him, as he ran his hands up and down her arms, pulling her to him "but you know our flight to Venice is tomorrow afternoon, and anyway you have more than enough in your life to handle at the moment".

Xander knew she was right, but it was going to be really hard knowing that after tomorrow she would still be in Italy for two days, in Venezia, before she really did actually leave for New York. With the twins coming out of hospital and his work commitments he was already crazy busy, he had five new projects all about to start construction now the winter was nearly over, but right now he would have done anything for a bit more time with Maria.

Xander did not think it was the right moment to say what was in his head right now, although he was planning to ask her if she would like to come back and visit, maybe early summer, in a couple of months' time. That way, he thought, the girls would be settled (he hoped) and he could invite Maria and her girls to the villa. He didn't think she would have driven all this way from Paris if she was not interested in him, and she knew about his girls now. Maybe she would like to come back to Italy. He really hoped so. Further than that he really had no idea what was going to happen, but he knew without a doubt he didn't want this goodbye, this second goodbye, to be the last time he would ever see her. He looked into her eyes, bent his head and kissed her so gently he surprised himself. He kissed her for a long time, they both just held each other, both feeling like time was standing still for them, as they explored each other's lips and tongues, gently, lovingly … until they were loudly interrupted by another small voice.

"Zio Xan what are you doing!!!!" cried Isabella in Italian, as she ran past them to the kitchen.

"ISA" Xander shouted loudly after her.

As Xander turned and shouted his niece's name, Maria watched his angular features and hawk-like profile with a really strange sense of déjà vu. She felt an irrational feeling of cold fear, which was totally out of context with the lovely evening they were having.

"ISA" he shouted again "go and ask your mama if dinner is ready, then go and get the others please".

Xander turned back to Maria, who was staring at him, a faraway look on her face.

"What?" Xander said "you look like you have seen a ghost".

"Yes sorry" Maria said, "sometimes I feel like I have known you for a very long time, I don't know how to explain it". The hair on her arms was standing up it was odd.

"Hey maybe we were lovers in a previous life" Xander joked and kissed her cheek, although he knew exactly what she meant. They both laughed and he took her hand and led her past his home office and up the stairs.

The second floor of the villa was beautifully decorated, Maria was impressed and told him how much she liked his house. Xander, pleased, showed her briefly all the bedrooms including the one that was obviously the twins new bedroom as it was full of paint pots, a mountain of cuddly toys, two white beds to be constructed and various bags of kids clothes.

"I think Isa and her sisters bought half of the kids stores in Firenze this morning" he smiled, looking at the pile of things "I just hope Alessandra and Celestina will like it here. They have lost so much and it is not like I have always been in their life. At least their mother got the chance to introduce me to them last month, otherwise I would be a total stranger" he looked horrified as he imagined what that would have been like. "In the hospital, you know the day I left Paris" he looked at her "that was only the second time I met them!"

"I know Xander" Maria said "I am sure they will settle, probably quicker than you think, I hope so anyway, for their sakes. And you seem a natural with kids, the way you are with Chiara's girls" she added.

He squeezed her hand and showed her around the guest suite which was gorgeous. All the bedrooms in the villa had beautiful marble en-suite bathrooms.

"Of course you have a choice Maria" he looked at her sensually "you can stay here, or you can stay in the only room you haven't seen ..." he led her down another corridor and opened the door to his suite. Maria was expecting to be impressed but..

'Just wow Xander!" she said.

The bedroom had a pale oak floor, a vaulted ceiling, an enormous bed with black, expensive looking bedding, a door that must lead to his dressing room and huge glass doors that led out to his private tiled balcony. She could see the stone balustrade that she had seen from the garden, and once again the image of being alone at the villa with Xander, being taken from behind as he held her against the balustrade flashed through her mind. She turned to him and he saw the desire in her eyes and pulled her to him, kissing her hard, before opening another door and saying "and this is my bathroom"...

What most people consider a "bathroom" was nothing like this. There was a huge marble-tiled walk in shower in one corner and a beautiful double sink area. The toilet was separate, through a door on the other side of the room. But in front of a full-length floor to ceiling glass window was a slightly sunken jacuzzi. Maria saw there was edging wide enough to take glasses and a holder for an ice bucket. The view from the jacuzzi stretched over the gardens out for miles over the rolling Italian countryside. In the middle and far distance there were cypress-lined roads with terracotta roofed Tuscan villas on the hilltops.

"Do you like it?" smiled Xander.

"I love the whole villa Xander, you have incredible taste" Maria said.

"That makes me happy you like it, you like my design" Xander murmured, taking her in his arms again, this time he bent down and easily picked her up. Maria laughed and grasped his neck as he carried her over to the bed and dropped her on it. He was so strong and muscular, she felt like a doll when he picked her up. He climbed onto the bed and crawled so that he was on top of her, keeping eye contact with her all the time, as his long dark hair fell around his face. Maria loved his wild, slightly neanderthal look, especially when he looked at her with such desire in his dark eyes.

"God I have missed you Maria" he breathed "it has only been two days since Paris but it feels like longer" he bent and kissed her hard on the mouth as she reached up around and ran her hands down his muscular back, digging her nails in as she reached down to his butt. He lowered his hips to hers, holding himself on his elbows as he thrust his tongue into her mouth. Maria could feel his huge erection through his trousers as he pressed himself against her and felt her pussy get immediately wet at the thought of him. He started to gently grind his hardness against her nub, through their jeans, as they kissed harder and more passionately.

Xander drew back so that he could undo his jeans and Maria helped him pull them and his boxers down to release his huge member. They took off their jeans and Xander drew a sharp breath as he saw her black lace panties. Suddenly the nights they had spent together came back in graphic detail and their mutual desire sparked even more strongly between them. The air was electric. She pushed him onto the bed, climbed on top of him backwards and leant forward to take him in her mouth. She opened her mouth as wide as possible to fit him in her mouth, his huge cock was already very hard and throbbing with desire. She started to move her tongue under his head, and he groaned with desire. She felt him behind her, grasping her butt, moving her panties to one side and pulling her down so that he could lick her pussy lips. She moaned, his member was thrusting into her mouth as he licked her. They had not had that much time together really, Maria thought, there was so much more they could do to each other, to pleasure each other.

As he was licking her he inserted a finger into her pussy, then two, her wetness giving him pleasure, she was so ready for him already. She wanted him as much as he wanted her. He found her g-spot and started to massage it with his fingers and heard her moan, her mouth full of his cock. He was so turned on he knew he could cum really quickly and tried to control himself.

"I want you to cum in my mouth" she said breathlessly.

"Maria I want you so bad" he groaned "I need to take you first".

Xander continued massaging her g-spot with his fingers, and then inserted a third finger, moving them around, stretching her pussy. Maria felt herself starting to build already, she was so turned on. Xander could feel her pussy stretching and throbbing, her lips growing swollen and ready for his onslaught. As he felt her get more and more turned on he pulled his fingers out of her, and as Maria let his heavy member fall out of her mouth and turned, he took her arms and pushed her fairly roughly onto the bed. They had not even taken their tops off as he grasped her ankles, forcing her legs apart and moved between her legs so that he was positioned to take her.

"Oh Xander take me, take me now, god I want you" she gasped.

"Are you ready Maria because I want you so bad, I can't control it" Xander breathed heavily.

"Take me Xander fill me, fill my pussy" she begged him, and as they held eye contact, he moved his huge member to her entrance and pushed his head into her. Maria gasped out loud as she felt the familiar feeling of being stretched to the limit by his size. With just his head inside her it felt as if her pussy had taken an orange inside of her. She was so wet for him she felt as if she was dripping readiness.

"Now Xander now" she commanded him.

Xander thrust hard up into her, filling her immediately so deeply she imagined she could feel his member in her throat as she gasped. He started to grind his hips into her immediately, staying fully inside her, laying down over her so that his pubic bone was pushing hard against her nub. Maria knew she was already close to orgasm and moaned as she felt his huge length penetrating her belly.

"Maria" he breathed and started to kiss her passionately as she grasped his butt.

Xander started to pump into her and Maria felt her engorged pussy lips being crushed then stretched as he drove into her over and over, pumping her pussy full of his cock as if he was trying to take her deeper and deeper every time he entered her. She started to groan as she felt herself start to build to a climax already.

Every time he thrust in and pulled out of her, his huge size was teasing her g-spot and Maria felt completely owned by him, as if nothing else existed except their bodies joined together in an erotic state of heightened sexual pleasure. She let her body start to build in waves …

"Xander I am going to cum already" she gasped.

On and on he pumped into her "cum Maria I wanna take you so hard".

As she felt her pussy take his huge length over and over she felt his member deep in her belly, thrusting up her and claiming her for his own. His movements were verging on violent, there was a desperation to his lovemaking.

"Yes yes" she cried out as she felt him bang into her and her pussy give way to wave after wave of orgasm. She reached around for his tight balls and felt his member become even harder. She knew he was close to climax.

As she orgasmed over and over and her body twitched as she climaxed, Xander bent and kissed her hard on the mouth.

"I want you in my mouth" she gasped.

He pulled out of her pussy, which was still in aftershocks of orgasm and put his huge head into her mouth. Maria looked up at him and the sight of her eyes showing the desire for him as she took his cock in her mouth just pushed him over the edge; he grasped his member as he pumped himself into her mouth using his fingers and felt his balls release the cum that spurted into her mouth in a hot stream of salty liquid. Maria felt her mouth fill with him, felt the hot cum shoot inside her mouth and, still keeping eye contact, swallowed it all as she gazed at him. Xander's muscular chest was still twitching from orgasm aftershocks as he looked down at her. She licked the remaining cum from his member and kissed it naughtily.

"OMG Maria" Xander breathed "what do you do to me?"

She just stared at him as he moved onto the bed next to her and they lay there together, facing each other. He kissed her, thinking that this was the first time he had ever kissed a girl who had just taken a full load of his cum into her mouth. He always found the thought erotic before orgasm, and wanted to kiss, sharing the cum, but right afterwards he normally never wanted to go anywhere near it. With Maria he just wanted to do everything. He could not get enough of her.

"I think the others might be expecting us for drinks" she whispered in his ear and he smiled.

"So have you decided where you might like to sleep tonight?" he kissed her and looked at her expectantly.

"Xander I think this enormous bed is way too big for just you …" she teased.

"That is settled then" he said "you are mine for tonight, my Maria who loves my blue birds" he laughed.

They stared at each other, both feeling the same thing without needing to put it into words - that it was near impossible the first time they met was six days ago. They felt as if they had known each other for far far longer. It was a sensation neither could explain.

They quickly put their jeans back on, and Maria went to find Lisette in the guest room, telling Xander they would be down right away for drinks before dinner. He kissed her again slowly and squeezed her hand, before leaving her to go back downstairs.

**

As Xander went downstairs his head was spinning. On the one hand he knew he had only known Maria for six days, but equally he did not want to let this beautiful woman out of his life. She must have so many admirers in NYC. He remembered in Paris how surprised he had been to find out she was single, all the men he had seen looking at her. A woman like Maria would not remain single long though, and he intended to speak to her later about his idea to come back and visit. It was a crazy idea that they could create anything together, with the distance between them, but wasn't that why he had left a 23 year relationship? To try to live his best life with no regrets? Xander's mind was made up.

▲▲▲

CHAPTER THIRTEEN

▲

A NIGHT IN TUSCANY

February 18

Maria and Lisette had showered and were changing to go down for dinner with the Sabatini family. Luisa and Carla were showering and changing in the other bedroom, having had a great time with the younger generation. They had already eaten (the lasagne was apparently "awesome") and were planning to join Marco, Gianni and the others for a film in the games room.

The younger girls had been allowed to stay up late. This last couple of days had been a series of new experiences and Chiara was not about to have a battle getting them to bed, when they wanted to stay up with the others. In any case it was not that often all the cousins got to spend time together.

Lisette was summarising what had happened in the garden earlier with Cristo …

"You kissed him already?" Maria squealed "you only just arrived Lise, what are you like?!"

"I know I know" Lisette replied, with a naughty look on her face "but we are leaving tomorrow and honestly Maria, you must understand, Cristo obviously has the same charm factor as Xander! You knew Xander for four days and you drove from Paris to Italy to deliver his dog so I don't think you can judge me!" she laughed loudly, then added "anyway you know what I am like, plus I will probably never see him again!!" Lise thought to herself it was a shame, as Cristo was the archetypal tall, dark and handsome. He was broodingly attractive with a bit of an attitude and as for his body, well, she hoped she might be checking that out later.

"I think it must be fate" Maria agreed "my trip to Paris, then you guys joining me, Cristo being here. I think we should go with the flow, enjoy the moment and not analyse too much".

They laughed and finished getting changed. Things were fairly casual so both were dressed in jeans and pretty blouses. Lisette's more lowcut than Maria's, she was proud of her "girls" as she liked to call them and liked to show off her breasts. Lisette at 5'9" was just taller than Maria and her blonde hair, blue eyes and curvy ass, coupled with her large breasts, meant she was used to getting a lot of attention from guys. Maria was shyer than Lisette and she enjoyed going out with her as you always knew the Amazonian Lise would draw people's attention!

They all made their way downstairs, where Luisa and Carla were immediately grabbed by Isabella and taken down to where the others were setting up the seating for all of them to watch the film. They had chosen a Bond film in English with Italian subtitles.

The amazing smelling lasagne was just being taken out to rest before being served and so they all gathered around the marble breakfast bar island in the kitchen for a glass of Chianti Classico before the meal. Xander had lost count of the number of times he had brought up more bottles from his wine cellar, but over the last two days it seemed to have helped the situation and everyone was feeling slightly happier about future plans, himself included. He was actually pleased that Maria's girls seemed to have broken the tension and taken the other kids' minds off what had happened. Marco and Gianni seemed more relaxed and he was relieved they seemed to be motivated to help him with ideas for the girls' arrival. They had even suggested getting swings and a climbing frame to put in the garden for them.

Lisette joined Cristo, Xan and Antonio while Chiara made a beeline for Maria, she wanted to talk to this adventurous American lady that Xan was clearly head over heels with. She hadn't seen him like this for a very long time. He didn't seem to be admitting it to anyone and certainly not himself, but Chiara could tell her brother was already hook, line and sinker. She thought it was very romantic. Maria seemed to be very close to him too. If you didn't know the story only started six days ago you would assume they were a fairly long established couple, Chiara thought. As for Cristo, he was always throwing himself passionately headfirst into situations and seemed to have taken to Lisette instantly. Chiara had a feeling how this evening might end for those two, and she smiled to herself. She loved hearing about her handsome brothers' latest conquests, it was better than TV. She suspected Antonio was about to have his own share of excitement soon, if he was really planning to leave Carmen.

They all clinked glasses and Chiara asked about her life in the States. Maria complimented Chiara on her English, which was actually quite good. Chiara's husband, Roberto di Arellano, spoke fluent

English as he worked in international business and they had decided their girls would have English lessons from an early age. Chiara said if they ever had more time together she would try and teach Maria some Italian! They talked about all sorts of things, including the impending arrival of Alessandra and Celestina and how everyone had taken the news. When Maria said she had two brothers, but no sisters, Chiara secretly thought how lovely it would be if something permanent happened with Xan and Maria. She really wanted a fun sister-in-law. She had never liked Xan's ex-wife (thank god the boys took after him not her) and Cristo's divorce had been so acrimonious nobody spoke to his ex either. As for Antonio, it was pretty much over with Carmen, his half-Spanish wife. If people think Italians are hot headed, Chiara thought ruefully, they should come and meet Carmen! Antonio would be much better off without her, she thought, although she sensed there was something else bothering him that he didn't want to discuss.

During the conversation Xander kept glancing over at Maria, she looked beautiful even though she must be tired. She seemed to be getting on really well with Chiara. He was happy with that, his sister was a very good judge of character and she seemed to have taken to Maria. Everything Maria did made him happy, he thought, and kicked himself for being so soppy. He needed to get focused on his projects and the twins' arrival, time would tell if he was destined to see Maria again, after tomorrow.

Lisette was entertaining the Sabatini brothers with details of life in NYC and had started to show them pictures on her phone (carefully, as her phone gallery was not for public consumption being a single girl) of some of their New York nights out together. They were all laughing and joking. Antonio asked who it was in one of the pictures and Maria heard Lisette explaining it was Luke their gorgeous gay friend. All the girls wanted the dark, sexy, half cast personal trainer, she explained, but he was not bi, he was totally gay and they hoped he would find true love one day, after a series of disasters. Luke was African American/white origin and had a very exotic look, as he had blue eyes, Lisette explained. This was all translated by Xander as Antonio was the only one of them who did not speak English at all well.

'Luke is soooooo gorgeous" Lisette explained loudly "he is soooo fit, he works out every day, all the girls are like, omigod, but he is just not interested" she laughed, then added "actually Antonio you would get on with him just fine, Luke loves cooking as well, you should taste some of the things he makes, they are divine" …

She went on to explain that Luke was expert at Latin American cooking as he spent his teenage years in Santiago because of his father's work.

"So Luke he speak Spanish?" Antonio asked Lisette in his best English.

"Oh yes he speaks Spanish fluently" Lise replied "but if any of you guys speak European Spanish you might think he has a funny accent" she laughed "it's kinda sexy though, when he speaks Spanish" she added, grinning.

"Toni speaks fluent Spanish" Cristo announced, "don't you brother" and so Antonio told Lisette he had a half Spanish wife. He explained (via Cristo's translation) that he had learnt the language as they visited Madrid two or three times a year to visit her mother's family; Alberto and Virginia were obviously bilingual. This impressed Lisette, all Europeans seemed to speak at least two languages, it was amazing. As she listened to Antonio speaking, she marvelled that all three brothers were so gorgeous. Antonio had the same dark stubble, slightly longer black hair than Cristo and was clearly super fit too. He had angular features like Xander but he had a gentler manner than the other two. But then Xander was the driven businessman and Cristo, well, nobody had an attitude like him, she thought.

Xander was watching Antonio's face as they discussed Luke and suddenly the penny dropped. They had all remarked upon Antonio's subdued mood and issues he was not discussing. He had explained he was having problems again with the volatile Carmen, which surprised precisely none of them, but there had been something more. *Was his brother gay?* Xander thought to himself.

They all sat down to eat and Maria thought to herself how extraordinary life was. Six days ago she had been spending her first evening in Paris, after bumping into Xander checking into the hotel. Now she was in his villa, in Italy, with his entire family, eating the most delicious lasagne and drinking Italian wine, it was crazy. Only this lunchtime they had been eating pizza with a view of the Leaning Tower of Pisa, before they came here. Tomorrow would have been her flight home to the States. Was it because she was in Tuscany with Italian people that everything seemed to gel so perfectly, taste so good? They were, she realised, not that far from the area of Italy where her father's family had originally been from, many generations back, before they moved to Argentina and then the States. Even her girls seemed right at home. She felt very zen and at ease with life.

The meal came to an end and they finished off with espresso and a shot of amaretto liqueur. Maria and Lisette thanked Antonio and the others for an utterly delicious meal and for such a warm welcome. Lisette said she felt tired and so Cristo suggested not very subtly that he would walk her to her room, at which point Lise caught Maria's eye and smirked ... they disappeared together and Xander, Maria and the others went into the main lounge with a last drink and continued chatting. Maria was feeling a bit hazy after the long drive from Monaco earlier that day and the emotional reunion, but this was very possibly the last evening they would ever spend together and she did not want it to end. She and Xander sat close together on one of the luxurious sofas and he put his hand protectively on her thigh, periodically moving his hand up and down her leg as they chatted with the others, as if it was completely normal she should be there. She could feel her pussy twitching at his touch and could not wait to be alone with him later in his suite.

**

After they had kissed in the garden earlier Cristo could not wait to be alone with Lisette again. She was the sexiest girl he had seen for a long time. Even he had noticed his black mood had lifted. He never felt really relaxed at the best of times, he knew he had issues. Sometimes he felt so angry inside and he descended into a nasty mood for days, particularly before a full moon. It was better since his divorce, apart from having Giovanni and Piero (as Pietro was known) he regretted marrying his ex. She had gotten pregnant as soon as they started dating and so they had married just before Giovanni was born.

Cristo tended to drink a lot if he went out in Firenze with his friends (most of them also divorced) and he had no problem flirting and picking up girls. He knew he was good looking, women just threw themselves at him and he had had plenty of sex over the last 18 months with different girls every few weeks, always with protection of course. He might be hot-headed but he was not stupid. The problem was they would always get too keen too quickly and bombard him with texts, wanting to meet up again. He really could not be bothered. He was more interested in the chase, once he had them he lost interest very quickly. He also never went for blondes normally, but Lisette's all-American blonde, blue-eyed look and energetic personality had had him interested from the moment she got out of the car earlier and assumed he was Xan. Her figure was magnificent, she was nice and tall and her breasts were very large. Cristo was the same height as Xander at 6'4" so although she was tall for a woman, he found her slim and graceful.

Lisette herself was fed up of being hit on by shortass guys who thought she would be interested just because they were (usually) wealthy. She never normally slept with guys this fast, she usually kept them chasing, but she would make an exception for Cristo, firstly because he was unbelievably gorgeous and secondly as she would never see him again after tomorrow. It was a shame, she thought, but they didn't exactly live near each other.

As they approached the guest suite Cristo asked if Maria had mentioned coming up to bed soon, to which Lisette laughingly replied she doubted Maria was going near her own bed tonight. As they glanced at each other they could sense the electricity and desire already pulsing between them.

They went in and as soon as the door closed Cristo turned and powerfully pushed Lisette back against it, grasped her face in his hands and kissed her hard, his dark stubble scratching her face but she didn't care. Lise had already reached around and pulled his shirt from his trousers and was gripping his back, pulling him towards her. She moved her hands down and grasped his rounded buttocks through his jeans; he was extremely muscular. As Cristo thrust his hips to hers, she felt the unmistakeable hardness of a large member. Maria had told her about Xander, being well endowed must run in the family she thought, with a jolt of anticipation. She felt her pussy get immediately wet at the thought of Cristo inside her.

They kissed passionately, at the same time undressing each other frantically. Cristo ripped off his shirt and threw it on the floor as Lisette undid his belt. He kicked off his jeans and shoes then picked her up easily and carried her through the lounge area into the bedroom. Lisette was impressed at his strength as she was not light! He threw her down onto the bed roughly and she looked up at him, standing there wearing just his white boxers. His enormous member was rock hard and bulging right up into the waistband of his underwear. He was huge, even contained it was the biggest cock she had ever seen.

Lisette sat up on the edge of the bed and pulled his boxers down to his knees. She gasped in admiration as his huge cock swung free, throbbing as she took it in her mouth. She looked up at him, her pretty blue eyes conveying her desire for him, his cock pumping in and out of her mouth, her pretty blonde hair cascading around her face. Cristo looked down at her and groaned as she proceeded to give him the most amazing blow job he had ever had and he had to stop her as there was no way he was going to cum that quickly. He reached for her top and pulled it over her head. Seeing her breasts for the first time, set off to perfection in her expensive red lace bra, he drew in his breath sharply, god she was sexy.

"Lisetta you are so beautiful, I want you" he breathed.

She loved the way he said her name "I want you too Cristo" she gasped as he pulled her bra down to expose her nipples. He took her full breasts in both hands, they were so large they escaped over his hands as he took one of her erect nipples in his mouth and started to suck on it hard.

"Omigod Cristo" Lisette murmured, as he moved across to her other breast. He reached around and unclipped her bra, allowing himself full access to her breasts which were heaving as she breathed fast with desire.

She ran her hands through his short dark hair and let Cristo do what he liked to her, the smell of his perfume had been driving her crazy all night, since they had kissed in the garden. He sucked hard on her nipples then moved down her body, still holding her large breasts in his hands, until he reached her nub … his tongue expertly found her clit and flicked backwards and forwards, feeling it harden, before taking it in his mouth completely and sucking rhythmically on it, over and over.

Lisette felt herself already close to climax, as his fingers found her nipples and squeezed hard, his mouth and tongue now moving down to her pussy lips. He let go of one breast and reached down, licking his fingers and inserting two into her dripping pussy. As he played with her clit with his tongue and moved his two fingers from side to side, Lisette groaned with desire. Cristo put a third finger in her pussy and expertly started to massage her g-spot, still playing with her clit with his tongue. Lisette had not been this turned on by a man, so quickly, ever, she thought. As his strong fingers writhed and massaged inside of her, her breast still gripped by his other hand, she felt herself go into waves of orgasm.

"Yes Cristo yes yes don't stop" she gasped as she came around his fingers.

Cristo pulled his fingers abruptly out of her orgasming pussy, licked them and then offered them to her to taste. Lisette gazed at him, her eyes filled with desire as she licked her own juice from his fingers.

"I want you now Lisetta" he commanded "open your legs".

Lisette moved further back on the bed and opened her legs wide as Cristo moved between her thighs, his member hard and pulsating. He pushed her thighs back slightly, his large hands holding her legs, and entered her with his head, playing at her entrance. She gasped as he invaded her body.

"Fuck me Cristo fuck me hard" she commanded him, knowing after his fingers had finished with her that her pussy was more than ready to take him.

Staring at her with pure lust in his eyes he held back his desire to thrust into her hard and instead pushed his huge member very slowly into her sopping pussy, stayed there a moment then withdrew slightly. He looked at his huge cock glistening with pussy juice then looked into her eyes, before ramming it hard right up into her. Lisette cried out as she felt herself being stretched and her belly being filled by Cristo's huge member and felt his large tight balls bang against her perineum before he stopped and just stayed inside her, moving side to side.

"Omigod yes take me" she cried.

"Lisetta you are gonna get filled with hot cum I am gonna take you hard" he breathed.

"Oh yes Cristo please yes" she gasped.

"You want it?" he asked.

"Now Cristo, now, take me" she was so ready.

Cristo pulled out of her so that he could see his rock hard cock in all its huge magnificent length, poised at the entrance to her pussy. He was amazed he could fit his member into a woman without causing pain, it was that thick and long. Her pussy was ready for him but it did not look as if it could take the length of him, he felt the familiar rush of carnal desire, a subconscious primeval need to thrust in, impregnate and fuck again. He looked her in the eyes as he leant over her and took a nipple in his mouth and sucked hard, still poised just inside her entrance.

"Omigod now Cristo stop teasing take me right now" Lisette was desperate for him.

"Ready Lisetta" he hissed.

And as he continued sucking on her breast he rammed his throbbing cock right up inside her, back out, right up again and thrust hard into her again and again. Lisette had never been taken this roughly by a man. Cristo was savage but he knew exactly what she needed. He thrust again and again right up into her, her pussy stretching and crushing at the onslaught. She reached down and felt her pussy lips being pulled so wide open then, as his member banged into her again, she felt her clit being pulled down as her pussy lips were pushed apart by his member. On and on he pumped into her, banging his member into her body over and over, harder and harder, feeling the end of her pussy every time he pushed right in. He couldn't last much longer he knew, he had been turned on all evening, but he wanted to make her cum again. Lisette was lying back, her legs wide open, her fingers had found his nipples and she was squeezing them hard. Suddenly he pulled out of her and flipped her over onto all fours.

Lisette had the most curvaceous smooth ass Cristo had ever seen, he just wanted to fuck her all night. She moved her ass provocatively and as he shifted behind her he could see her huge breasts swaying underneath her. He reached around and grasped her breasts, whispering in her ear.

"I am gonna take you from behind. You want me now?" he breathed.

"Yes yes Cristo take me, give it to me, give it to me" she was breathless with desire.

Cristo positioned himself behind her, and before entering her pussy he licked a finger and inserted the full length of it hard into her ass. Lisette cried out, then screamed his name into the pillow as he opened her pussy lips with his fingers and started to push his member into her, slowly this time. She could feel, as it slowly stretched its way inside her, his cock moving over her g-spot and opening her deeper and deeper. With the finger inside her ass Cristo could feel his own cock moving inside her pussy. He was moving slowly as he was so close to orgasm he could have cum immediately. When she didn't think he could fit any more of his cock inside her, he stopped and started moving in a circular motion before starting to fuck her again hard. Lisette gasped as he pumped and pumped into her from behind, faster and faster. She could feel herself building for another orgasm, could feel his finger fully in her ass.

"Fuck me Cristo fill me fill me" she groaned.

Cristo could feel himself ready to cum, he couldn't hold himself much longer. He rammed into her over and over, the sight of her curvy ass turning him on so much he felt his balls tightening ready for climax. His member slid easily in and out of her tight wet pussy, and he felt himself ready to discharge his sperm. He banged harder and harder into her, moving his finger in her ass at the same time, listening to her begging him to fuck her.

"I am gonna cum Lisetta are you ready?" he hissed.

"Yes Cristo now now" Lisette felt herself building for a massive orgasm.

His member hardened again as his balls tightened and he fucked her violently over and over, overcome with desire, repeating "I'm gonna fuck you" over and over. On and on he rammed deep into her as he felt it rising in him. As Lisette started to scream "yes yes" into the pillow and started to quiver with orgasm it pushed him over the edge and he heaved his member hard up her, feeling his hot sperm shooting up through him and deep into her pussy. He cried out loud and pumped several times, feeling himself discharge fully into her, before pulling out his finger from her ass and pulling out of her gently. She felt his sperm flow hotly out of her and down over her pussy lips and clit. She watched it drip onto the sheet under her. She felt totally stretched and violated, he was so huge and so rough, but at the same time he fucked in such a sensual way he did not seem brutal.

He turned her over and lay down beside her, her blonde hair spilling all over the pillow as they kissed. Cristo had calmed down immediately now he had cum, he reached for her and held her tight. He knew he got a bit rough at times, he had a passionate nature, but now he just wanted to hold this blonde American girl tight. He kissed her so softly all over her face and stroked her pretty hair gently with his fingers. Lisette smiled at him and snuggled into his hard, muscular chest. She had already sensed this passionate Italian with the bad temper was a big soft teddy bear inside. Cristo had not planned to stay in her room, but after her long journey, the stress of the last couple of months for him, the dinner with copious amounts of wine, then wild satisfying sex, they both fell asleep within a couple of minutes.

**

The others had finished off the bottle of liqueur and were talking in the lounge.

Downstairs the younger generation were still in the games room. Chiara and Antonio wished Maria and Xander goodnight then went downstairs, Chiara collected her three (who were extremely tired but still insisting they wanted to stay up) and they asked the teenagers to head to bed no later than 3am, before going to bed themselves. All the teenagers seemed to be getting along just fine with each other.

Alone in the spacious lounge, Xander kissed Maria gently and told her he wanted to ask her something.

"Of course Xander, what is it?" Maria smiled at him, feeling herself melt as he looked at her with his gorgeous dark eyes. He really was the most handsome man she had ever seen.

"Maria, I know you are leaving tomorrow afternoon, but I do not want this to be a final goodbye" he took her hand "we said goodbye two days ago in Paris and I accepted that I would never see you again, but now, for me things have changed. I want to give us a chance, I don't know how it would work out, but …" he hesitated "… would you like to meet again, maybe in a couple of months? Come back to Italy?" he looked at her intently.

Maria felt a jolt of happiness and butterflies in her stomach. She had been hoping he might say something like this. She too had accepted, sadly, that after Paris they would not see each other again, but after the huge journey to bring Zeus home and spending more time with him … he was right things had changed. It had got quite serious between them very quickly and she still couldn't shake the feeling they somehow already knew each other. Maybe this is what it felt like when you met your soulmate, because she could not describe the feeling. She certainly had not felt like this with James, although things had been hot in the beginning, she had never felt they were soulmates. Nothing like this connection she had with Xander.

"I would really like that Xander yes" she squeezed his hands and as she did so Xander felt a huge weight lifted from his shoulders. He was so pleased. He had not been entirely sure what she would say. His situation was not exactly "normal" for a single guy. He reached for her and took her in his arms, holding her tight, before pulling back and looking at her.

"Maria I have another question, I would really like you to come with me tomorrow morning to the hospital, to see Alessandra and Celestina, would you come with me?"

Maria considered this. On the one hand the poor girls had had enough of new faces and tragic news, they didn't really need to be introduced to yet another stranger. But, she felt somehow that it was a good idea. She also realised that Xander would appreciate her support. They had an evening flight booked to Venice so they had plenty of time. She also realised, that although Xander had only asked her to come back and visit, that he must be feeling the same closeness as she was. Otherwise, there would be no way he would have suggested meeting his little girls. What was it with this gorgeous Italian man, she thought. Strangers until six days ago when they met in Paris. Life was unpredictable that was for sure. She thought her girls would be happy spending more time with the Sabatini cousins tomorrow morning, they all seemed to have got on really well, even given the language barrier.

Xander could see her contemplating his question and added "one day Maria I would really like to show you Firenze. I will take you to the Uffizi Gallery, the Pitti Palace, the Duomo, the Ponte Vecchio. You will love Firenze I know. But tomorrow I can only take you to the hospital!" he smiled at her, hoping she would agree. Maria had such a good "vibe" about her, he didn't know how to explain it. He knew the girls would like her, even though they could not communicate properly unless he translated. He was looking forward to getting them home from the hospital. The pink paint decorating would easily be finished tomorrow, Antonio and Cristo were building the beds and all the kids were in charge of arranging the toys and clothes for the twins. Isabella had suggested making a welcome banner with her sisters and making name pictures for the door to their room. Everyone was coming together to make sure they made it as nice as possible for the girls' "homecoming". To their Papa's home they had never even seen, he thought ruefully. He had not gone into the flat they had lived in with their mother, only met them outside, but he had not got the impression it was very big. He hoped they would like the space in their new home, and the garden of course. With summer coming he would have to make sure they could swim, he was sure they would like the pool.

"OK Xander, I will come with you, if you think it is a good idea" she smiled at him.

For an answer he just leaned in and started to kiss her, slowly, holding her face between his hands. After a while the kiss grew stronger, more urgent, and she felt the familiar insatiable desire growing stronger between them.

"I think it is a very good idea" Xander murmured "and I have another very good idea what I would like to do with you right now".

He got up and pulled her to him, putting an arm around her shoulders as they walked out of the lounge and up the stairs.

$**$

Maria went into the guest suite quietly to get her things, smiling at the thought of Lisette and Cristo who was presumably still here, given his shoes and clothes were all over the floor in the living area. They were well suited she thought, knowing Lisette's personality and what she had seen of Cristo today.

Xander went straight into his bathroom and turned on the jacuzzi lights and jets, leaving the rest of the room in darkness, before getting a bottle of Moët out of the hidden fridge. He put it in an ice bucket on the side of the jacuzzi, with two champagne flutes, before going back into the bedroom and taking off his shoes.

Maria returned with her case and as soon as she was inside the door Xander took her case, dropped it on the floor and pulled her to him hard. They kissed passionately, the same immediate desire they had had in Paris, but more intense this time. He thrust his tongue into her mouth, urgently exploring her tongue and nibbling on her lips. He felt a wild need to possess her, stronger than before, if that were possible. They were on borrowed time, under normal circumstances she would have been preparing to leave northern France 1400km away, he would have been sorting out his life here in Italy. Fate had brought them together again, even if it was just for tonight. He didn't want to waste a second with her. Maria grasped his buttocks, pulling his hips to her, running her hands up his muscled back. She felt herself already wet with desire, her clit was throbbing for him.

Xander had planned to invite her into the jacuzzi for champagne, but that idea went totally out of the window as he kissed her harder and harder. He grasped her hand and led her over to the bed, pulling her blouse over her head roughly then unbuttoning his shirt. Maria was already undoing his jeans, running her fingers over his length as she felt the hardness through his boxers. He threw her onto his huge queen-sized bed and pulled off her jeans so that she was left wearing just a sexy dark purple lace bra and panties.

"Maria" he breathed "you are so beautiful I want you so much".

"Xander I need you inside me, I want you" Maria said, breathless.

Xander knelt over her face, his enormous member arching and throbbing. She opened her lips so that his head entered her mouth, as her tongue moved slowly back and forth under his head. She then licked the full length of his shaft again and again, licking his head each time. Xander groaned. If he let himself go he could cum so fast, too fast, so he moved down and started to kiss her breasts and suck on her nipples, so hard she cried out. She felt the familiar immediate twitch in her clit when he pulled on her nipples and could feel her pussy throbbing and moistening for him.

Xander moved down her body, pushed her thighs open and started to lick her clit, before putting his whole mouth over it and sucking hard. His fingers reached up and found her nipples and squeezed on them. The sensation was unbelievable, so intense and Maria knew she was going to orgasm fast, she could not help herself.

"Omigod Xander yes, yes" she whispered heavily.

"You want me Maria? You want me inside you tonight?" he said, squeezing her nipples hard with his fingers as he looked up at her.

"So much" she breathed.

Xander started to lick her pussy lips as Maria gasped with desire. Then, he put his hands on her thighs and pushed her back still further, opening her legs, and putting a pillow under her ass. He thrust his tongue into her pussy then moved down and started to lick from her pussy, over her perineum down to her ass. He flicked his tongue over her ass again and again, before using long strokes with his tongue licking back from her ass up to her pussy lips. He licked with long strokes over and over again and Maria felt herself being overcome with desire. He had not even entered her and she was ready to orgasm.

Xander felt himself so hard he knew he would not be able to control himself for long. He stopped licking her pussy and put two fingers, then three, then four, inside her, pushing into her and opening and closing his fingers.

"Turn over Xander" she suddenly commanded him.

He rolled over onto his back and it was her turn to kiss him, then move down his body. She kissed his muscular chest with its light covering of dark hair, licked and nibbled his nipples, then moved down the bed to where his cock was arching between his legs and Xander groaned as she once again took him in her mouth, stretching her lips open to fit him in. This time she moved right down so that she was between his legs. She made him bend his legs and pushed his thighs up with her hands so that she could lick all down his shaft, taking his tight balls in her mouth. He moaned as she sucked them gently, before moving her tongue under them to where she could feel the thick root of him, licking him firmly as she moved her tongue down to his ass.

"Oh yes Maria that is so good si si" he breathed, the feeling was so intense. It was a long time since any woman had licked his ass, he loved it, and with Maria everything seemed amplified. The feeling was electric, so forbidden but so sensual.

Maria kept her hands on his thighs and licked backwards and forwards over his ass, pushing her tongue a little into him. She felt him tense as she then licked firmly over and over from his ass, up to his balls and up his shaft. Again and again she played with his ass with her tongue, licking him over and over. She inserted a finger a little way into his ass and took each of his balls in her mouth. Xander was trying to hold himself back, the feeling was unbelievable.

He stopped her and pushed her over roughly onto her back, four fingers once again entering her hard as he kissed her.

"I need to take you Maria, I can't control it" he gasped, looking at her.

"Take me now Xander, take me hard" Maria was breathing heavily.

She felt herself lengthening and stretching for him inside, her pussy lips already swollen in anticipation of the hard pounding she knew was coming.

Xander felt her pussy so wet and ready for him and he pulled out his fingers, sucking the pussy juice from them and massaging some onto his cock. He wanted to own her hard and fast but he didn't want to hurt her, he wanted to make sure she was ready.

Her hips still held up slightly by the pillow, he leaned over her body and once again kissed her passionately. She could taste her own juice as he kissed her and licked around her mouth with an animal passion.

She could feel his huge member touching her entrance as they kissed and her pussy throbbed with desire for him.

"Now Xander, please" she said.

"I am gonna fill you Maria, are you ready" he groaned.

For an answer she kissed him hard and as their tongues writhed together, Xander positioned himself at her entrance and this time did not just enter her with his head. He knew she was ready. As he crushed her mouth with his, he thrust his huge member hard right up into her pussy and heard her cry out as she was kissing him. He felt himself at the end of her pussy, so he moved in a circular motion slightly to make sure she was entirely stretched open for him, then pulled out and proceeded to pump her so hard he shocked himself at his desire. He thrust up her again and again, filling her so full with his hardness.

Maria just felt entirely owned by him, as if her whole being was one open pussy, being taken by the most enormous member she had ever seen. Nothing else existed in that moment except their desire for each other. As he plundered her hard and fast, pumping her over and over, she knew she was going to orgasm fast. She could sense him already close too, as she cried his name.

"I am going to cum Xander" she breathed as she felt the waves building.

"Me too I can't hold it" Xander was breathing raggedly, he could feel his sperm building deep in him, ready to shoot through his hard cock into her.

As he continued heaving into her over and over, she reached down and felt the familiar width of him between her legs, and her forced-open swollen pussy lips. She touched her clit, which was hard with desire. With her fingers she could feel his huge and very hard cock sliding in and out of her pussy, crashing into her as he pumped, his full balls banging against her perineum. She opened her legs as wide as she could, allowing him to fill her as deeply as possible. With the pillow under her ass he was penetrating even deeper into her and she was again amazed at the depth of her pussy and how she could take his huge size into her. She felt her orgasm building as her pussy started to grasp around his member, pulsating and tightening around him.

Xander felt her pussy tighten and heard her start to cry out as her orgasm started. He let himself go, he had to cum, he thrust his rock hard member hard again into her as he felt his sperm moving through him, and with one final deep thrust he felt himself discharge a fountain of cum into the depths of her.

"Yes Xander yes yes omigod" Maria cried out as she orgasmed over and over, her whole body quivering.

"Ahh si si siiii" Xander cried out loudly as he came, thrusting with aftershocks.

He collapsed onto her, holding his weight on his arms as he kissed her again, more tenderly this time. He rolled off her and took her in his arms. They lay together face to face, pressed tightly against each other, as she felt his hot love juice pouring out of her and down over her leg and ass.

"I think the champagne is chilled by now" Xander joked, looking intensely at her, "would you like to shower and have a jacuzzi, with champagne, my bella ragazza?"

"That sounds perfect Xander" Maria replied.

They washed in his beautiful marble shower and then got into his jacuzzi. The feeling of the relaxing warm bubbly water, after such unbelievably hot sex, felt amazing. Xander opened the bottle and poured it into the two glasses.

"Welcome to Italy" Xander said with a naughty smile.

"Here's to Zeus arriving home in style" Maria joked as they clinked glasses.

They laughed and sipped champagne, looking out of the huge glass window. With the only lighting in the bathroom being the coloured lights of the sunken jacuzzi, they could see the lights from other villas on the hilltops in the distance.

"Watch" said Xander, turning off the lights completely and jumping out to open the large window.

The weather had changed, and the night was very clear. They could see the stars in the cloudless springtime sky above. What a view from your bathroom, Maria thought. They could see Orion and the "seven sisters" of Pleaides quite clearly. Xander slipped back into the jacuzzi, took a sip of champagne, turned her face to him and kissed her. She felt the champagne trickle from his mouth to hers, as it had done on the night of Saint Valentine's, in her suite in Paris.

Even if it was gone midnight and officially February 19, it was still only five days since their first night together. It felt like so much longer. They gazed up at the stars and galaxies so far, far away, and their eyes were drawn not to the impressive Orion with his belt of three stars, but to the distant Pleaides constellation. Xander reached for her hand under the water and they glanced at each other, his dark brown eyes meeting her greeny-blue gaze in an intense moment of subconscious knowing. They both felt a deep, distant connection, the same unexplainable feeling Maria had had earlier when Xander had shouted for Isabella, but without the fear. Under the warm water, with the cold night air on their faces, they looked at the stars together and without putting it into words they felt so right together, as if they belonged together and always would. Always had...

After a while, Xander reminded Maria that he had promised her a massage after her drive from Monaco ...

**

Xander led Maria back into the bedroom and told her to lie down on the bed for a back massage "out of this world" as he put it. Xander climbed astride her, rubbing massage oil into his hands. The smell of the oil was gorgeously sensual and as Maria felt his large hands start to spread the oil all over her back, in strong sweeping motions, she felt all tension start to leave her body.

Xander closed his eyes as he massaged her back, working on her spine and moving up to her shoulders. With his eyes closed he had always had a strange sort of ability to be able to sense where any pain or tension was being held. Maria's shoulders were a bit tight and he carefully used his fingers and thumbs to work the oil into her skin and work the knots out of her shoulder muscles.

"I am not sure thousands of kilometres in my car in two days were good for your shoulders my Maria" he joked, pummelling her firmly.

"No you're right" she replied "I need a massage a day for at least a week after that journey".

"Well in May you can have a lot more than a massage a day" Xander murmured suggestively "would you like to come and stay for three weeks?"

"That sounds like bliss" Maria replied, imagining what three weeks with him would be like, if they were this close after only six days.

He was concentrating on massaging her but Maria could feel, when he leant forward, his cock, flaccid but still certainly not small, swinging between his legs. Every time he leant forward it lightly brushed against her legs and ass. Although she was now very tired she still felt a twitch of desire run through her as Xander touched her body.

As he came to the end of the back massage, Xander leaned forward, his cock again brushing against her ass, as he whispered in her ear …

"I think I will just check if your legs have tension".

"Yes please do that Xander" Maria murmured sexily.

Xander put some more body oil on his hands and started to massage her buttocks sensuously, before moving down to her legs. He ran his hands down her legs, working on her muscles, before moving back up and parting her legs. He could feel himself hardening again at the sight of her gorgeous firm ass and perfect pussy, looking enticing between her legs. He could see her pussy lips were still pink and slightly swollen since his onslaught earlier, before the jacuzzi.

He put some oil on his finger and, after massaging back and forth over her ass, slipped a finger inside. With the other hand, he played with her pussy lips then inserted two fingers up inside her. Maria moaned into the pillow as she felt her pussy start to moisten for him. He inserted a third finger and started to push in and out with them, while moving his finger in her ass from side to side. Maria didn't think there was anything this Italian couldn't do to her, whatever he did turned her on so much she was overcome by a strong primeval need to be taken hard by him.

After a few minutes he pulled out all his fingers and, his cock already fully hard, started to play at her ass entrance with his huge member. He watched as his huge head pushed against her tight hole and crushed it slightly. It didn't look like it could possibly fit. He was unbelievably turned on. He had imagined this while they were in Paris. He had also imagined this several times after he came home, while soaping himself in his shower, he remembered.

Maria was still face down, her breasts and nub already stimulated as she was lying on them and the pressure was exciting her. She had had anal sex a few times in her life and had enjoyed it, but never with a guy as big as Xander. She was not sure his huge member would fit inside her.

Xander moved his cock and moved it down to her pussy entrance with his hand. He pushed slowly inside her until he was deep in her, moving slightly but staying fully in her. He leant over her back and licked her ear, before whispering…

"Maria I want to take your ass, do you want me to?"

"Yes Xander but go slow, very very slow" she breathed, feeling his cock pulsating deep in her pussy.

Xander pulled her up onto all fours, reached underneath her and grasped her breasts. Squeezing them, he started to pump slowly in and out of her pussy with his huge member. Maria could feel him sliding in and out of her, she was so turned on she felt as if her pussy was dripping wet. He withdrew slowly and reached over to the drawer beside his bed and retrieved a bottle of lube and some anal beads. Maria felt her clit twitch in anticipation. She had never imagined she might have anal sex with someone who had such a huge cock.

Xander put a lot of lube on her ass, on his fingers and yet more on his cock. You could never have too much lube for anal, he knew, and he didn't want to hurt Maria. He inserted a finger into her ass again, and moved it in and out, then slowly added a second finger as she moaned into the pillow. With his two fingers he moved them in and out gently and then moved them apart, to open her slightly, turning them so that her muscles relaxed slightly and opened.

"Omigod Xander yes" she breathed.

"I will go very slow" Xander said, he had never been so turned on in his life as right now.

With his fingers held apart, he squirted a bit more lube directly inside her, before withdrawing his fingers slowly. He inserted the anal beads and heard Maria gasp as they entered her, each one bigger than the last. He moved them in and out slowly, then he positioned himself behind her ass, pulling the toy out gently. He again played at her ass, pushing slightly as Maria gasped. His enormous member, glistening with pussy juice and lube, still didn't look as if it could fit, he thought. He pushed a bit harder and Maria gasped again, it felt sensuously painful.

She moved so that she was supporting herself on one hand, then reached around and held one butt cheek open with her other hand.

Xander watched as he saw her ass open slightly, and put one of his hands the other side, to pull her open a bit more. He breathed in sharply, brimming with desire. All the times he had spent with Maria were the most erotic he had had for a very long time, he just wanted to possess her everywhere. He had already pumped his cock into her mouth and she had swallowed his sperm earlier that evening; he had already taken her pussy hard, now the only hole left to possess was her ass and he really really wanted her.

"OK Xander take me now, I am ready" Maria murmured.

"Are you sure" he asked her.

"Yes yes take me now, take my ass" she breathed.

As they both held her ass apart, he held his cock and pushed his head between her ass cheeks, applying more pressure to her ass. This time, as she pulled with her fingers to keep herself open, he pulled the opposite way with his fingers. He was overcome with desire to thrust hard into her, it was that erotic, but there was no way he would do that. He continued applying more and more pressure and watched as the head of his cock stretched her open and started to disappear into her body. Maria cried out into the pillow as his huge head stretched her tight ass muscles wide apart.

"Are you OK" he asked.

"Yes yes go on please fill me" she gasped.

He pushed harder and felt his head entirely inside her. The pressure on his shaft was unbelievable, so intense. He knew he would not be able to control himself for long being this tight inside her. Maria had let go of her ass cheek and he realised she was playing with her clit. She then inserted two of her own fingers inside her pussy. Slowly slowly Xander pushed more of his length inside her, as yet he had not drawn back out. There was lube everywhere, his member was a tight fit but it was entering her slowly.

Maria was so turned on, with her fingers in her pussy she could feel his massive size from the inside as it made its way up her ass.

"Omigod Xander that is so good" she breathed.

"Maria I want you so bad" he managed to gasp, the feeling was so intense.

"Ohhhh" she cried out, as he continued to enter her, deeper and deeper.

She felt him so deep inside her; her pussy was so squashed by the pressure from inside her ass her fingers felt tight in her.

Xander pushed on and on, slowly, until with one final thrust which made Maria cry out, he had fully entered her. She felt his tight balls touch her pussy lips and knew he was totally up inside her ass. The feeling was so horny, she loved it. She started playing with her clit and knew she would not take long to orgasm. She felt stretched but it was not painful at all, which, given his enormous size, was quite surprising, she thought. Just thinking about his enormous member, now entirely inside her body but up her ass, made her pussy become sopping wet.

"Are you ready Maria I am gonna take you now" he said raggedly.

"Yes yes take me" she replied, breathless.

As he pulled out ready to start pumping her, she felt her ass muscles protest slightly and cried out but told Xander not to stop. He pulled slightly out then pushed in again, pumping her slowly, deep in her, before then pulling further out. Then, he pulled out of her nearly totally, watching as his lube-wet cock was released from her body. He pushed back in, harder than before, and started to move rhythmically in and out of her. Maria was still playing with her clit, one finger in her pussy. The feeling of Xander plundering her ass was like nothing she had experienced before. Her ass had got used to the idea and it felt so sexy and forbidden being taken by him like this.

The tightness was driving Xander crazy, he knew he couldn't last long. He pushed deep in her, felt his balls against her lips, then pulled very slowly completely out of her. He looked at her ass, now pink and open for him, although as he watched it started to close again. Quickly he added more lube and put his head back in her, making her gasp again, and pushed hard up her. She was ready now, he knew he was not going to hurt her.

"Fuck me Xander fuck my ass" she gasped.

"You are gonna get it, I can't last long" he breathed.

He looked down at his cock again, positioned with his head already inside her ass, her ass cheeks so rounded and sexy. He slapped her ass, making her cry out, and then drove into her really hard. His cock disappeared fast up into her ass and he felt the tightness around his shaft. It was so so good. He pulled out then started to pump hard, driving hard into her with every thrust. Harder and harder he took her, Maria had to stop playing with her clit and support herself on both hands, he was pumping so hard. Xander could not control his desire, he needed to take her. On and on he rammed his huge member deep up inside her ass.

"Yes Xander yes fill me up fill me up" she cried.

"Maria I am gonna cum" he gasped.

She felt herself building for orgasm and started to play with her hard clit again, the feeling of being possessed anally by this beautiful man with the massive cock was pushing her over the edge. She felt the waves building.

Xander was watching his huge member going in and out of Maria's ass, watching her stretch every time he pulled out, then crush as he drove back in. Harder and harder he gave it to her, holding onto her hips with his hands so as to drive in as deep as possible. He would make her his, in every hole, he thought, overcome with desire to ravage her.

On and on he banged into her, listening to her crying out for him to fill her. The feeling was incredible. He felt his balls tingling and knew he was about to cum. He pumped in deep over and over, feeling the sperm moving through him ready to erupt into her. Maria felt herself totally taken by him, her ass full of hard cock. She wanted his cum up inside her so bad, she was close to climax herself. She held her breath to intensify the orgasm. Violently he pumped harder and harder until with one final thrust he felt the sperm surging through his cock and deep into her ass. He cried out, thrusting with the aftershocks as he discharged all of his cum up her, as she played with her clit, bringing herself to a massive orgasm at the same time, her pussy quivering and pulsating as she felt his massive cock fill up her ass with his hot cum.

They were both breathless as he pulled slowly out of her, and they lay down side by side. Xander took her face in his hands, checking she was OK, before kissing her.

"Omigod Xander that was incredible" she said.

"I actually don't have the words to describe how good sex is with you" Xander said "not even in my own language. Unbelievable".

They smiled as they kissed, then lay together for a while before showering.

As they got into bed it was very late, tomorrow they would be shattered, Maria thought.

Xander lay on his back, his strong arms circled around Maria who was snuggled into his chest.

Completely spent, they fell asleep immediately.

**

Deeply asleep, Maria dreamt of star constellations and swimming in purple-coloured bubbling water, with Xander joining her as they played under a huge waterfall. But then Xander turned into some sort of angel or bird, he had wings and took off over the water…. she felt a frisson of fear that she might not see him again and she had to find him no matter what the cost.

▲▲▲

CHAPTER FOURTEEN

▲

ARRIVEDERCI
THE SECOND GOODBYE

February 19

Maria woke first, they can't have been asleep that long she thought, as it was only just hinting at getting light outside. Softly, so as not to disturb Xander, who was sleeping with his back to her, his black hair tousled on the pillow, she crept out of bed. She slipped on Xander's black bath robe then tiptoed across the wood floor, quietly opening the door to the balcony. It was chilly, but the sky was clear and it promised to be a warm sunny late February day in Tuscany when the sun came out.

The balcony was tiled, with a pretty balustrade slightly above hip height. She walked to the edge where it looked out over the countryside behind the villa and she could see in the half-light, under the dark turquoise blue morning sky, all the gorgeous cypress trees and rolling hills. In the garden below her she saw the fountain, with its pretty waterfall and angel statues, it really was beautiful. She could hear faint low chirping, a just-woken-up warbling noise coming from the birds in the aviary. She couldn't see them as one of the large palm trees on the terrace was so tall its huge fronds were masking that side of the garden. It also masked the view to the balcony from all the other rooms that faced this way, she noticed, except the window to Xander's bathroom. She raised her arms above her head in a contented stretch and breathed in deeply, imagining the fresh morning air cleansing her lungs as she breathed in and out. She felt a deep sense of belonging to Italy and especially Tuscany. She felt very centred and calm.

"Cosa stai facendo la mia bella ragazza" Maria jumped as she felt Xander's strong arms around her waist as he spoke softly in Italian and kissed her neck. She felt his hard chest muscles pressing against her back. He was so gorgeously tall, she felt so protected by him.

"I am admiring the view from your beautiful villa" she explained, leaning back against him, then tilting her head around so that she could kiss his sensual lips.

He turned her to him and kissed her softly, holding her face in his hands. For someone so large and incredibly physically strong he could be so gentle, she thought. He was passionate beyond belief and verging on violent in the bedroom, but always so careful of her. She loved the way he treated her, like a strong warrior King protecting his Queen. She was going to really miss him after they left today.

"So which part of the view do you like best?" he murmured, turning her back around to face the countryside, so that he was behind her. He pushed her forwards slightly so that she put her hands on the balustrade.

She felt him pull the bathrobe up so that the cool air moved against her ass. Xander moved his hands over her ass, gripping her cheeks, before moving around to her stomach and running his hands down to her nub. Maria gasped as he started playing with her clit and exploring her pussy lips with his fingers. Her pussy and ass still felt used from the night before, and as she remembered what they had done last night she felt her pussy get immediately wet with desire.

"Wait there" she heard Xander say, as he moved a little way back from her.

"Lean forward and put your hand on your ass" he instructed. She moved sexily, tilting to one side, one hand on her ass cheek, as she realised he was taking photos of her.

"Move your legs apart slightly" he commanded, and Maria leant forward over the balustrade, parted her legs and put both hands erotically on her ass. She could hear Xander muttering in approval as he was being turned on just watching her.

He took a couple more photos then, as she was still facing the view, came back and pressed himself against her. She could feel he was still wearing a tee shirt but had taken off the shorts he had come out in. She could feel his rock hard cock pressing against her ass. She moved up onto her toes and moved her ass provocatively, leaning forward over the balustrade. Xander inserted two then three fingers into her still wet pussy and started massaging her g-spot. With the other hand he ran his fingers over her ass ...

"You are so beautiful, I wanted to take you here since Paris" he murmured, letting his fingertip enter her ass very slightly and kissing her neck again.

"Xander I want you" she breathed quietly, although she doubted any of the others had their windows open at this hour of the morning.

Xander bent his knees slightly and, taking his huge member in his hand, positioned it at her entrance. She could feel the pressure on her pussy lips and swayed her ass to help guide him in. She felt the familiar stretching as he pushed his huge head into her, very slowly, then continued to push into her, letting his member be engulfed slowly by her pussy.

Maria felt herself being invaded again; she could feel him entering her body so deeply she felt as if her belly were entirely full of him. She leant further over the balustrade and opened her legs wider, to let him take her completely. She felt him reach the end of her, then gasped as he pushed still further in, until she felt his tight balls touch her pussy lips.

They were both being very quiet, it was unbelievably sensual, they could hear the early morning noises of the countryside, the birds in the aviary and the water tinkling in the fountain just below them. The dark turquoise sky was lightening slowly, the last stars disappearing.

Xander started to take her slowly, moving in and out of her pussy with long sensual strokes. He wasn't building up to pounding her like he had the other times, she realised, he was taking his time and, if it hadn't only been a few days since they met, she would have said he was making love to her.

The fact that they could not make any noise heightened the electric feeling between them. Maria felt herself being taken over and over again by his hugeness, pulling right out of her pussy slowly then thrusting back in. On and on he rhythmically moved in and out of her. He reached around and started to play with her clit with his fingers, then massaged her pussy lips.

Xander could feel his cock disappearing into her as his fingers pushed against her pussy lips. He could hear her groaning quietly *"oh yes oh yes omigod"* and it turned him on so bad. He moved his hands up under the robe and found her breasts, squeezing them then pressing her nipples hard between his fingertips. He knew he was driving her crazy. He also knew he couldn't last much longer. Even after over an hour of sex last night, he wanted her all over again now. He couldn't get enough of her. Her pussy felt so tight around him, he started to move faster in and out of her.

"Oh yes Xander don't stop" she whispered, her pussy grasping at his member as she felt herself already building for orgasm.

He was still squeezing her nipples and she reached around to cup his full balls in her hand. They were full to bursting again, this guy was so hot, so sensual. She let go and moved her fingers to her clit, playing with herself as she felt her pussy full of his thick cock that was smoothly pumping in and out of her, slipping in and out of her pussy lips. Every time he thrust into her, crushing her pussy inwards, she could feel her ass as it was pulled towards her pussy. It had taken such a pounding last night, she was amazed they had had such hot anal sex and she had not hurt afterwards.

"You are gonna make me cum Xander" she breathed.

"You cum my beautiful Maria, cum around my cock" he hissed quietly.

"Tell me when you are close" she said, it turned her on knowing he was close to orgasm, it pushed her over the edge.

"I am close already" he murmured, continuing to drive deep into her, over and over. She felt her pussy so open and ready for him, but it was still a tight fit due to his massive size, she wanted him like she had never wanted any other man. The connection between them was so intense. On and on he thrust up into her, plunging his cock deep inside her, she could feel the waves building.

"Now Xander yes yes" she cried quietly.

He let himself go and started to take her harder and faster, feeling the familiar tingling and the desire that overcame him when he knew he was close. He looked down at her gorgeous curved ass, listening to her begging him for more. As he remembered taking her ass the night before it pushed him towards climax and he drove hard up her, deeper and deeper. Maria pushed back against the balustrade as he was pumping her hard, she felt her pussy start to melt and quiver in waves of orgasm. As she cried out softly as she came, Xander drove harder up into her, and again, before discharging his cum deep in her. He reached around and held her tightly to him as he finished pumping his cock up her, with the aftershocks of his orgasm.

"Maria you drive me crazy" he breathed "every time it's different, every time it gets hotter."

"Omigod Xander that was incredible, again" she agreed.

As they went back inside, Maria could feel his hot sperm running down her legs, it was such a sensual feeling. She felt totally owned by this gorgeous Italian man.

They headed into the shower together before getting ready to go and get breakfast...

**

Back in the guest suite Luisa and Carla were sleeping. They had come up to bed the night before very late, after all the teenagers had spent most of the night in the games room watching films and chatting. They had all come upstairs together and as Carla had opened the door they had all seen Cristo's clothes strewn all over the floor. They had all laughed and joked about the adults behaving like teenagers the whole evening, it was really funny. They had already promised to stay in touch after the girls left today.

Marco and Gianni were planning a party for May, when hopefully the girls would be coming back from the States to see them all. The new twins would be here then, it still seemed so strange, but they supposed by May they would be used to the idea.

**

In Lisette's bedroom, Cristo woke early and couldn't remember where he was. Then he quickly recalled the previous night, as Lisette moved next to him, and he saw her blonde hair all over the pillow. He had not had a night like that for a long time, he thought, not with someone he wanted so badly. He was getting a little bored with the single life, the constant chase then losing interest once he had them. He was craving something different, but he had not been able to put his finger on quite what he was looking for. His chain of gyms kept him extremely busy and he had just started to invest in property in Firenze, but since his divorce he had been agitated and restless, worse than usual.

He reached for Lisette and stroked her arm, before moving his hand down her body and running it over her hip. He felt her move back against him and move her gorgeous ass sexily and he reached around and grasped one of her full breasts. He moved his other arm under her so that he had access to her other breast. He felt himself get immediately hard as he massaged her huge breasts in his hands. They were truly magnificent, heavy but firm, her nipples hardening as he touched her. He moved over her slightly so that he could take a nipple in his mouth and sucked and sucked on it. He heard Lisette groan quietly and remembered that Maria's girls were asleep in the bedroom the other side of the guest suite. He couldn't stay long, he needed to leave before they got up.

"Good morning Lisetta" he whispered, before moving athletically over her and looking down at her amazing body.

"Morning Cristo" Lisette smirked at him, reaching for his hips and pulling him towards her.

They kissed passionately, Cristo thrusting his cock against her nub as they explored each other's mouths with their tongues. Lisette felt herself moisten as his huge member dipped into her pussy, which was still full of his juice, and then rubbed up and down over her clit. God this guy was stunning, she thought, as she reached down and started to play with his cock. It was already oozing pre cum, this guy was just about as excitable as you can get, she thought.

"I want you Lisetta" he murmured "I want you now".

"Take me Cristo take me hard" she breathed.

He reached down with one hand and thrust two then, finding her already sopping wet, four fingers into her pussy, moving them in and out and sideways fairly roughly. Lisette cried out softly each time his fingers thrust searchingly up into her.

Cristo stopped abruptly then parted her legs, pushing on her thighs to open her up for him. He moved quickly to position himself at her entrance and inserted his head into her pussy. Lisette breathed in sharply as he then moved over her body and started to suck on her nipples again, still holding himself just inside her pussy.

"I love your tits Lisetta they are magnifici" he said, sucking hard.

Lisette felt her clit twitch every time he sucked on her, she wanted him so bad, but he still wasn't entering her.

"Now Cristo, I want you" she ordered him.

"I am gonna take you hard Lisetta" he breathed quietly, raising himself up so that he was between her legs. She looked at his hard, muscular chest and felt her pussy start to quiver as she got wetter and wetter with desire. Cristo was stunningly attractive, so strong.

Cristo looked at her and with the most savage animal look she had ever seen on a man, he suddenly rammed his huge cock right up inside her. Even though she was totally ready for him, he was so rough. God she wanted him though. She grabbed his ass and held him as he pumped into her, harder and harder. She lifted her head and looked down at her pussy where she could see his massive member plundering her. Cristo looked intensely at her with his dark eyes, she felt totally at his mercy, he was so big and muscular, a man mountain. She opened her legs wider for him and let him do what he liked to her.

"Yes Cristo yes" she gasped, quietly.

"I want you Lisetta I want you now I want you all the time" Cristo was overcome with desire.

He drove hard into her again and again, then flipped her over onto all fours.

"You are my little bitch Lisetta I am gonna fuck you" he hissed as he entered her from behind.

"Take me Cristo" she gasped, as he banged into her. She felt herself building already.

Roughly, he turned her over again and wrapped his arms around her so that she couldn't move.

"I would like to tie you to the bed my sexy Lisetta" he whispered into her ear.

Totally trapped by his arms they kissed passionately, so hard Lisette felt her lips bruising, as he moved his heavy member between her thighs, entered her and started to fuck her hard at the same time. Faster and faster he drove into her, crushing her pussy lips as he took her. She could feel herself building for a huge orgasm and felt him harden again, ready to shoot his load into her.

"Yes yes" she gasped into his ear "fuck my pussy I'm gonna cum".

Cristo could not hold himself back, he banged harder and harder into her, feeling the end of her pussy every time he drove in. He could feel her pussy starting to quiver with orgasm and it pushed him over the edge.

"Yes Lisetta yes" he cried out into the pillow.

She felt his massive member harden again, as her pussy dissolved into wave after wave of orgasm and with his final thrust she felt him discharge his load right up inside her in a fountain of hot love juice. They were locked together, Cristo gripping her so tightly she couldn't move, as they quivered in the aftershocks of climax together. They stayed like that for a couple of minutes, both breathless, then Cristo rolled off her and lay on his side, propping himself up with his elbow so he could look at her.

"Lisetta you have to promise to come back and visit with Maria. If you don't I am gonna lock you up so you can't leave" he joked, gazing at her pretty face and lovely blonde hair.

"The idea of being your prisoner isn't a bad one Cristo" Lisette replied, kissing him "but OK I promise". She had only thought she would have this one night with him, but the idea of several weeks (nights) with this utterly gorgeous Italian guy ... the mind boggled.

Cristo felt a strange emotion, he felt really happy. He didn't remember the last time he felt this relaxed and happy. He enjoyed life, he liked to go out and have fun, he was sociable, but he always had an underlying anger at life, he never could figure out why. But right now that had gone, he felt a lightness that was unusual. Then he felt bad that he had noticed how unusual it was. Was he that grumpy and bad tempered normally? He wondered about himself sometimes.

"OK Lisetta I am gonna leave before the girls wake up" he said, rolling athletically out of bed and quickly retrieving all his clothes from the living area.

She watched him get dressed, admiring his incredible physique, muscles in all the right places. And as for his cock, she watched how it bulged in his jeans as he zipped them. He was so sexy.

"See you at breakfast then" she said, giving him a sultry look.

Cristo kissed her then quickly left and Lisette went back into the bedroom before taking a long shower in the gorgeous marbled en-suite bathroom. This villa was beautifully designed she thought, and wondered what Cristo's house looked like, he had told her he lived in Florence, or Firenze as he always called it. She bet he had a real minimalistic bachelor pad.

**

The light was streaming into the east-facing kitchen. Zeus was lying on the tiles again, he loved the underfloor heating. The smell of Italian coffee brewing was pervading the whole house and the chatter of voices filled the air. Breakfast was a busy affair, everyone was up at the same time, drinking coffee, eating pastries or toast. The teenagers were all at the breakfast bar and the adults sat at the table.

Maria noticed Lisette was sat between Cristo and Antonio and she was showing them more photos of when they had had a Mexican night at Luke's apartment in NYC.

"So it was like, soooo delicious" Lisette was saying "we had chilli and fajitas and tequila cocktails, we all stayed, then for breakfast Luke made chilaquiles it was so good".

Maria remembered how Luke had made the typical Mexican breakfast, it had been amazing. There were also pictures of them all in Mexican fancy dress so Lisette had everyone laughing.

Xander kept his hand on Maria's leg under the table the whole time they were eating breakfast. They were both well aware that it would be quite a long time before they were eating breakfast together again.

They all agreed that it did not seem like they had only arrived the previous evening, so much seemed to have happened. They had had so many new experiences and seen so much on the drive down here, that it seemed to Maria that she had been away from home for about three weeks at least.

The teenagers disappeared together, making the most of their final morning together, the little girls holding Luisa and Carla's hands.

**

Leaving the villa for the hospital, as they crunched slowly down the drive and out into the Tuscan countryside, Maria was enjoying the view from the car a lot more. Yesterday had been the last leg of their huge journey and she had not been able to fully appreciate the stunning landscape. It was truly beautiful and it was so nice to be back in the Maserati, with Xander driving. She glanced at him, thinking of their trips to the Bois de Boulogne in Paris with Zeus. Xander looked at her, his full lips in a sexy smile, his dark eyes boring into her. Maria's heart turned over as she looked at him, and at his angular profile as he turned and concentrated on driving down the winding hillside. He was a stunning looking man and the chemistry between them was out of this world, she thought. What timing, or destiny, had brought them together in Paris, so far away from both their homes, she didn't know, but she was certain they had been meant to meet.

On the drive he told her more about what they would see in the ancient Italian city of Florence, or Firenze as he always said, and where he would take her in May. He also promised to take her to the beautiful towns of Volterra, San Gimignano and the famous Siena, which were not too far from his villa. As he told her about the exciting Palio, the centuries-old bareback horse race that takes place in the centre of Siena twice a year, he suggested that if she wanted to see it then she would have to come back in July or August as well, glancing suggestively at her. It all sounded amazing, and Maria told him she would love to.

"Providing we get on OK when I come back in May of course" she said smiling "we might not like each other after three weeks together" she joked.

"True, so we need to spend a lot of time together, to see for sure" he joked, his voice tailed off as he gazed intensely at her.

They arrived at the hospital and made their way into the building up to the floor where the girls were sharing a room. They were holding hands as they walked up the corridor, but Maria let go as they entered the room. No need to create more questions for the girls.

As they approached the twins, Xander went straight over and kissed them both on the cheek, stroking their hair as he greeted them and asked how they were. They were immediately interested in who had come in with their papa. They gazed curiously at the pretty lady he had brought with him. He introduced her as a very good friend who had two daughters of her own and they said "buongiorno" in small voices.

Maria realised Xander was right when he had told her they looked like him. They were adorable, really beautiful with long dark hair and big brown eyes. They looked like Marco and Gianni in some of the black and white prints back at the villa, when they were about the same age. She admired the way he was so sweet with them, he seemed very relaxed and attentive.

They spent 30 minutes with them, at one point two nurses came in to check the twins' blood pressure and their dressings, as apart from the whiplash trauma from the collision both had been injured by the broken glass.

As Xander started to get up and clearly was telling the girls he would be back later, Maria asked Xander if he could tell them she had a present for them. She asked him to explain she had not known she would be meeting them, so this was only a small token, but she had something for each of them.

Their little faces lit up at the word "regalo" even though he had said it was a small one and they started to chatter rapidly in Italian. Xander looked confused then questioned what Alessandra had said, before translating for Maria.

"She says they never got presents, nobody bought them presents before" he explained with a slightly shocked look on his face "she said even on their birthday they didn't really have many presents".

They exchanged glances quickly and Maria looked at the twins. Alessandra was just staring at her, Celestina seemed to be the quieter one and was looking decidedly downcast at the conversation. Neither seemed to be able to believe somebody they had never met would give them a present. She wondered what their life had been like, up to now.

Xander told Maria in English that he had no idea what their day to day life had been like, before he met them. Since the end of the affair nine years ago, he had only met with their mother just the once, three weeks ago, when he met the girls for the first time. He had also never seen where they lived. He was as confused as she was.

Maria reached into her handbag and pulled out two New York Knicks caps, one white with black lettering and the other black with white. She handed one to each of them and they squealed with delight as they tried them on then looked at each other. It must be like looking in a mirror, Maria thought, as she smiled at them. She asked Xander to explain the caps were from her two girls. They said "grazie tanto" hugging the caps as if they were afraid they would be taken away.

"Xander can you ask them if I can give them a kiss goodbye?" Maria asked, suddenly feeling very sorry for these poor little girls.

"Certo" he replied and spoke to the twins in Italian.

They were nodding and smiling so Maria approached the beds and bent to give them a kiss on the cheek. Alessandra then Celestina both immediately reached up and gave her a cuddle, which she returned, holding them to her and stroking their hair as she spoke to them in English, telling them she hoped she would see them again soon. When Xander translated this they both replied that they wanted to see the nice lady again, and her daughters, to say thank you for the hats. Maria was touched, they were so cute, the poor little things. From the conversation about the presents, she imagined they were going to be slightly overwhelmed at the contents of their new bedroom and all the gifts arranged by their new cousins! She wished she could see their faces when they came home.

As she thought this, she checked herself, as she had subconsciously thought of them "coming home" when of course the villa was nothing to do with her! Just calm down and see where this leads, she told herself. You have Venice to visit for two days, then the trip back to NYC and back to "normal life". She would see what the future held with Xander in a few months' time and, she laughingly thought to herself, what with Xander in Paris, road trips with Zeus and getting distracted in his Italian villa, she hadn't exactly had the week of assessing her life and deciding on her next steps, as she had originally planned!

Xander was watching her with his girls. Maria was amazing he thought, she seemed like such a natural with them. Obviously she was a mom and had two girls of her own, but it was a long time since Luisa and Carla had been that age and he remembered her comments in Paris about enjoying having older kids. But she seemed very at ease with Alli and Celli (as they had told him they liked to be called) and they seemed to like her. He really hoped their homecoming would go well. They were clearly much better physically, and able to come home fairly soon, but he had already spoken with the doctors about having regular sessions with a child psychologist booked for the next twelve months at least. He had also enrolled them into a school in Firenze near his offices, so he could drop them off and pick them up. They would be coming to his office after school a fair bit, he imagined, as he worked late some evenings, but he had already decided on a side office he would convert for them, where they could do drawing and play while they waited for him.

He had been thinking about an idea one of his employees had proposed at their last annual review meeting. She had suggested having a creche or nursery for kids up to 3, as it was tricky finding childcare. Now he had two young ones of his own he appreciated the juggling many single parents who work full time have to do, and he decided to get started on that project, set it up and give his employees reduced-cost care for their kids. Apart from that he would try to work a bit more from his home office, especially during the holidays. For his business trips Cristo had offered to come and stay at the villa if Xan had to go away for a few nights. He would broach the subject of looking after the twins when he was away with Gianni and Marco, but only after they had got used to the idea of the girls living with them.

They put on their coats and laughed with the twins, who had put their caps back on and were messing about with each other. Xander explained to Maria they had told him they loved fashion and were joking how well their new hats went with their hospital gowns! Maria made a mental note to bring princess dresses with her when she came back to Italy. They seemed quite lively when they left and Maria was glad she had met them.

Next time, she thought with a warm feeling in her heart, she would see them at Villa Volterra, with their pretty bedroom, new climbing frame and their papa and brothers. What a huge change for them it would be, but she was sure they would be happy with their new life. Luisa and Carla had loved Xander's three nieces and she was sure they would get on well with the twins too.

They made their way back to the car and set off for the villa where Antonio was preparing lunch for them all.

**

Antonio had made spaghetti carbonara for lunch, which was the best Maria had ever tasted. They all laughed and chatted together.

Soon though, the time came to load their cases into the car and leave for the airport. Luisa and Carla were in the kitchen, making a fuss of Zeus, before saying "arrivederci" to all the cousins. Marina and Gabriella, the youngest, were in tears as they hugged them. The boys and Virginia were all smiling and saying goodbye, but they were going to miss these cool girls they only met yesterday. Apparently, their papa had invited them all to come back and stay in May, so they were all exchanging cellphone numbers, Snapchat and IG user names, to keep in touch until then. The boys were joking that they hoped Lisette was going to come too, as their uncle Cristo wouldn't be very happy otherwise!! They all smirked and laughed together. Isabella and her sisters had already got their mama to absolutely promise they could come back up from Roma and visit when Luisa and Carla came back. They could go in the pool then, as it would be nearly summer. The teenagers were planning a huge pool party.

When they all said their goodbyes Luisa and Carla thought it was hard to believe that they didn't all know each other before yesterday, when they arrived with Zeus. Now they all felt like they had known each other for ages. They had only got about 3 hours sleep, so none of them were firing on all cylinders as they all hugged each other goodbye, all promising to learn more of each other's language before they saw each other next.

After countless hugs and promises to message each other, the girls got into the Maserati. Lisette managed to let go of Cristo and got into the back with Luisa and Carla.

Maria hugged Cristo, Antonio and Chiara and kissed all the younger generation, telling them how nice it had been to meet them all. Chiara had made sure to get Maria's number and they were going to keep in touch. Maria had promised she would speak better Italian when she came back. They had all talked about early May being a good time to come back to visit, in ten weeks' time. They all wished her an amazing two days in Venezia.

Xander was already in the driver's seat as Maria got into the front.

"I am so glad you are driving again" she said, remembering the unbelievable distance she had driven in his car. Thinking about it now, it had been a really insane idea. But what a great time they had ended up having here at Villa Volterra with Xander and his lovely family. Xander smiled at her and put his hand on her leg as he shouted something in rapid Italian to Antonio about his plans for that afternoon, telling them he would be back later.

"Let him go Lise" Maria joked, as Cristo was kissing Lisette through the back window, accompanied by hooting and whistling from all the kids standing on the drive.

They pulled away and Maria felt a wrenching feeling in her gut as they drove away from the beautiful villa. She felt strangely attached to Tuscany even though they only arrived yesterday! They had walked around the garden again quickly after lunch, seen the beautiful macaws flying in their huge aviary. It was such a peaceful place, with stunning views, she felt better knowing she would be coming back.

They seemed to arrive at the airport very quickly. Why was it, Maria asked herself, that when you know you have a limited time with someone, time seems to speed up.

They checked in and moved through to the customs area. Lisette suggested to Luisa and Carla that they should go through customs first and let Mom say goodbye to Xander in peace. The girls seemed to be happy with this idea, both had been non-stop messaging on their cellphones, since they left the villa. Clearly the Sabatini cousins had become close friends already!

As they went through and their bags went through the scanners, Maria turned to Xander. He put his arms around her and pulled her to him, holding her tight to him. She put her face against his chest, he was so tall she was a whole head shorter than him. She felt so protected, she didn't want to leave. Xander didn't want to let her go. He knew it was going to drive him crazy knowing she was only a relatively short distance away in Venice, for two days.

"Maria I am going to miss you" Xander said, holding her and looking into her eyes "I am going to be insanely busy with work and the twins, but I am really going to miss being with you, it does not seem like you only arrived yesterday does it!"

"No, it doesn't, and I am going to miss you too Xander, a lot" Maria said, smiling slightly sadly at him.

"Thank you again for bringing Zeus all the way back from Paris for me!" he laughed "it was an insane thing to do but I am so glad you did it, my brave bella Maria".

"Well I still can't quite believe we did it" Maria said.

They both laughed and they held each other tight again, before Xander bent his head to kiss her slowly, tenderly, their tongues moving sensuously together. They kissed for a long time and eventually they could hear the unmistakeable sound of Lisette the other side of customs calling "get a room!!"

They pulled apart, looking into each other's eyes. She had to leave now. Maria suddenly felt very emotional and her eyes filled with tears.

"No no my Maria don't cry" Xander said in his gorgeous accent.

"I will message when we land, in about 30 minutes!" Maria tried to joke.

"I want you to have an amazing visit to beautiful Venezia and send me pictures" Xander said "specially any private pictures you might want to send me" he added with a sexy smile.

They kissed once more, then Maria walked away, placed her bag on the conveyor belt and walked through the body scanner.

As she collected her bag and went to join the others, she glanced back one last time.

Xander was still standing there, staring at her. She could feel him, she could sense his agitation as she left. They had such an uncanny bond. She kissed her hand and blew a kiss at him and in reply he made as if to grab the kiss, then put his right hand over his heart … the gesture was so familiar, Maria thought, smiling, but then she realised with a strange feeling that Xander had never done that until now. So why did it seem so familiar? One last lingering look and she turned to join Lisette and her girls.

**

As the plane took off about 45 minutes later, Maria glanced down out of the window. She could see the beautiful Tuscan landscape getting smaller and smaller as they climbed, the cypress trees, the hills and valleys, the terracotta roofs with numerous turquoise pools in the gardens.

"See you soon I promise" she whispered under her breath, as much to the Italian land below her as to Alexander Sabatini, the Italian in Paris she never expected to meet, or fall …. she caught herself, and told herself not to be so ridiculous.

She turned to her daughters and Lisette, who all seemed to have expressions on their faces matching how she felt. Luisa and Carla had not stopped messaging the others since they left the villa. Carla had apparently got very friendly with Alberto, Antonio's son and Maria had a suspicion that Luisa liked Gianni, the quieter twin.

What a whirlwind time they had had! It was going to be very strange knowing Xander was actually only a fairly short car journey away for the next two days.

After virtually no time, it seemed, the passengers were asked to fasten seatbelts in preparation for landing. They were approaching Venice Marco Polo airport and their first ever visit to Venezia, the "City of Canals" or, as the Italians call their ancient city, "La Serenissima".

▲▲▲

TO BE CONTINUED…

A novella prequel (Book 1) will be coming summer 2021...

AND a sequel (Love in Europe - Book 3) to follow...

▲

Thank you for reading PARIS

♥

About the author

Sofia di Siena is a native English speaker living in France and speaks four languages. She adores Paris, hence the initial setting for her first novel Paris. She also has a passion for Italy and has spent time in Venice, Florence and Rome. She is a single parent with two daughters and is committed to bringing them up as strong women. She is passionate about empowering women and standing up for women's rights, particularly single moms, who often have too much on their plate to handle already AND they are trying to set up a business (or write a book!). She believes everyone should follow their dreams and live their best and fullest life. If one door closes (or several slam shut in your face at the same time) keep going, keep strong, another door that is meant for you will open ...

♥

Published by Sofia di Siena

© 2020 Paris

All rights reserved. No part of this book may be reproduced or modified in any form, including photocopying, recording, or by any information storage and retrieval system, without permission in writing from the publisher.

The scanning, uploading and distribution of this book without permission is a theft of the author's intellectual property. If you would like permission to use material from the book please contact : sofiadisiena777@gmail.com

Disclaimer:
This is a work of fiction. Many of the names, places, characters and incidents are either the product of the author's imagination or are used fictitiously. Any resemblance to actual organizations, events, locales or persons — living or dead — is entirely coincidental.
© 2020.

Printed in Great Britain
by Amazon